THE INGRAM INTERVIEW

Also By K. B. Dixon:

A Painter's Life

Andrew (A to Z)

The Sum of His Syndromes

My Desk and I

The Ingram Interview

a novel

K. B. Dixon

3B

Baffling Bay Books

Publisher: Baffling Bay Books

ISBN 978-1-7346759-3-1

1 3 5 7 9 10 8 6 4 2

For Sandra Jean

1

WHERE ARE YOU?

I am at Fairview Court.

WHAT ARE YOU DOING?

I'm sitting in a folding chair at the back of the community room—this morning a makeshift auditorium—watching rehearsals for this month's talent show. I am dressed in my usual sweatshirt and wrinkled khakis. If you were watching, you would have seen me sneak a peak at my watch (a doubloon-sized thing purchased twenty years ago from the Swiss Army) because even though I have tried often to change my ways, I remain one of those loathsome retentive types obsessed with time and I have—in thirty-one minutes—a meeting scheduled with the perpetually gracious Catherine Cain.

WHAT IS FAIRVIEW COURT?

Fairview Court is—or has been for the past four months—my home; what, in today's euphemizing parlance, would be called a "continued care facility." It is a crossbred thing (like a jackalope or a tangelo)—half hospital, half hotel.

WHY ARE YOU HERE?

I am here because I am old—or oldish (62)—and have apparently suffered some sort of heart attack. I say "apparently" because the boys in white have not been able to reach consensus on a definitive diagnosis—a thing I try not to let trouble me more than it should. All we know for sure is that I went to bed one night feeling fine, and I woke up the next morning ruined. I collapsed on my way to the bathroom.

IS IT A NICE PLACE, FAIRVIEW?

Let's just say it is not an un-nice place. A little small perhaps and banally decorated in beiges and muted mauves—it offers a full set of amenities. There is a pleasant dining room, a staff of medical professionals, weekly housekeeping and laundry services, art classes, exercise classes, craft classes—etc., etc., etc. It also offers a guarantee: a guarantee that my uniqueness will be honored and that I will be respected for the special individual I am.

AND?

And it comes with a certain saccharine ambience—an institutional commitment to the ceaseless expression of an unwavering conviviality.

WHO IS REHEARSING?

I have been watching Quinton Kohl, our resident hypnotist. His new best friend (and current stage patsy), Theodore, does not seem to be particularly susceptible to Quinton's mesmeristical charms. He will not bark like a dog—not yet anyway. But Quinton is nothing if not hopeful.

Right now on stage though is Edward Manning. Edward is trying to put the finishing touches on a polish-up of his juggling-on-rollerskates routine. He is seventy-one years old and comically vain. He flaunts his sense of balance every chance he gets because he is one of those needling weasels who thrives on the envy of others. It is excruciating to watch my provisional friends over there—Simon, Richard, David—try to turn their feelings of unalloyed hatred into believable facsimiles of sincere admiration, but in craven deference to the guiding feel-good principles of the place, they invariably do. I think Edward gets away with this heartless tease in part because of his jowly face. Everyone thinks he looks sad; they do not want to add to his troubles.

I can see Edward has gotten a little rusty since his last outing. His steadiness is not quite so insultingly certain. I can also see from that look of grim resolve that he is committed to recovering his form. He is determined to show us all that he is incomparable. He is determined to show us all that he is a phenomenon. I tried to talk him into skating a little closer to the edge of the stage. I told him if he truly wanted to impress us, he would introduce an element of danger into the act—but predictably enough he ignored me.

DO YOU ENJOY THE TALENT SHOW?

The honorific is, of course, an aggrandizing misnomer. There is rarely, if ever, any real "talent" on display here. The vestiges of something that was almost a talent are occasionally exhibited—the vocal stylings of the Barbra-Streisand-besotted Joan Nagel, for instance—but this is usually the most that one can hope for. Generally speaking these shows are terrible as entertainment. I know there are people who can make a whole evening of terribleness, but I am not one of them. Terribleness loses its diversional value for me pretty quickly. I become annoyed and cruelly bored.

BUT THE PEOPLE HERE AT FAIRVIEW DON'T ACTUALLY COME FOR THE TERRIBLENESS DO THEY?

No, they don't. They are not the people I am referring to. Those people—the ones who can make a whole evening of terribleness—are another set altogether, a small urban clique who embrace a frivolous, unnatural, esoteric sensibility. Here at Fairview one's attitude toward the talent show is considered a signifier of one's attitude toward a general frame of mind—an endorsing, unconditionally welcoming frame of mind.

It has nothing to do with the acts being good or bad, entertaining or not. It's all about spirit—the spirit with which the performers approach the performance. If they approach it with the right spirit, then everyone (except me, it seems) approves unreservedly.

AND IF THEY DON'T APPROACH IT IN THE RIGHT SPIRIT?

Well, that is one of the things that makes Edward's juggling-on-roller-skates routine so interesting. He pretends to approach his performance as required, but he doesn't do a very convincing job of it. The delight he so clearly takes in generating feelings of jealously remains too obvious. The audience—which wants nothing more than to be unambiguously supportive—invariably finds itself just the wee-est bit conflicted.

WHO JUST SAT DOWN NEXT TO YOU?

That emaciated specimen is Donald Taylor. Donald is my neighbor. He resides across the hall from me in the ominously denominated (or is that denumerated) Room 666. He wants to argue with me about my demeanor, about my "pandering passivity." Don, you see, is a closet cynic. He is on my side in this. He thinks I am making it too easy on them. It is a remarkable thing about Don—the purity of his hypocrisy. Desperate not to make waves himself, he encourages wave-making by others whenever he can.

WHAT IS THIS MEETING WITH MS. CAIN ABOUT?

Catherine is my counselor. We are all assigned one when we arrive. This meeting is about my being kicked out of Fairview. It is Catherine's job to conduct the "exit interview." It is supposed to make us both feel better about my eviction.

YOU HAVE BEEN ASKED TO LEAVE?

Yes.

WHY?

Mostly because of my attitude, which the bedizened powers have described as being basically not very good—my attitude and my distinct reluctance to socialize. I am not a team player, and it appears that this has been getting some people down—people who signed on here because they were assured they would be kept up. There have been complaints. I have cast a pall in the dining room with my habitually brutal critiquing of the weekly dinner menu. Here in the community room I am considered standoffish. In the rec room I am viewed as overly aggressive at the ping-pong table.

DO YOU FEEL BAD ABOUT BEING ASKED TO LEAVE?

No, not really. They did a nice job of it—very professional. It was one of those compassionate expulsions. They were sorry, but various evaluations made it clear that we were just not meant for each other. These things happen. Neither of us was at fault. Our differences, though minor, were nonetheless irreconcilable. They didn't ask me to leave so much as explain to me why it was that I simply couldn't stay. If I feel bad about anything, it is the inconvenience, the disruption. I just wanted to be left in peace to work on my book.

BOOK?

I'm writing something that looks and feels very much like a memoir. Having some sort of "apparent" heart attack has gotten me interested in this benighted genre. I have tentatively titled it *Assisted Living*.

SO YOU DON'T MIND LEAVING FAIRVIEW?

No, I don't mind leaving. I have no attachment to the place and only a slight attachment to a couple of the people here—Roger Davis, for instance, and maybe Elliot Reich. The problem, of course, is that I haven't been able to find a new place yet, which is why I am going to be staying for a bit with Michael Berger, an ex-student of mine. He has offered to put me up while I look for something else.

MICHAEL BERGER?

Michael is a peculiar young man. He makes art movies—short, incomprehensible things that no one wants to watch. Confusing things—things without much in the way of conventional cinematic oomph.

WHAT ABOUT YOUR FAMILY?

I am a modern man; I don't have much of one. There is an ex-wife, Emily, and a son, Richard. I am in negotiations with Emily, but at the moment they are not going very well. As for my son, he lives in France. We haven't gotten along for quite some time now . In fact, we have made not getting along the cornerstone of our current relationship—in other words, we are estranged.

THERE ARE ISSUES?

The gist of Richard's complaint is that I am a selfish bastard and that if I had not been one, he would not be what he is today—which is poor, lonesome, and borderline dysfunctional. My reply to this complaint has been to suggest that he blame his grandfather. If his grandfather had not been the selfish bastard he was, I would not have been the selfish bastard I am, and, consequently, he would not be the poor, lonesome, etc., etc., etc.

WHAT DOES RICHARD DO FOR A LIVING?

For the last few years Richard has been working in a vineyard. He grows grapes. He sells them to a co-op that makes a relatively inexpensive burgundy—the sort of thing you might use to wash a frozen dinner down with. Better than everyday, but not good enough for special occasions.

2

DO YOU LIKE CATHERINE'S OFFICE?

No, I don't. The devotion to an aesthetic of unrelieved innocuousness is oppressive. There are no colors, no corners, no contours. Nothing stands out except the fact that nothing stands out—a thing that seems to bother no one.

CATHERINE LOOKS A LITTLE UNCOMFORTABLE.

That's guilt, I think.

GUILT?

The first thing she wants to talk to me about is my audience yesterday with Matthew King, the chicly goateed head of Fairview. She feels bad, but she was compelled by a sense of duty to be honest in her report to him. (New admittees have a report done on them after their first ninety days.) This isn't just my "exit interview";

it is Catherine's exculpatory allocution—a thing gone through in the hope of making her feel better about doing what she is supposed to do.

WHICH IS WHAT?

In addition to acclimatizing us and addressing our general concerns, it is Catherine's job to evaluate us psychologically. She did this—over the course of four or five brief interviews—with a standard checklist of questions. Did I see myself as someone who was talkative? No. Did I tend to find fault with others? Yes. Did I worry a lot? Yes. Was I quiet? Yes. Was I trusting? No. The theory is simple enough: if they have a better idea of who we are, they would have a better idea of how to help us fit in.

AND THE ASSESSMENT?

It was basically what you would expect: that I am an intransigent, moody, analytical loner.

WHAT DID THE CHICLY GOATEED MR. KING HAVE TO SAY?

It was Mr. King who delivered the velvet-gloved, corporate-speak kiss-off. After a soft-sell recap of Fairview's maudlin mission statement, he tiptoed toward the point—namely, that there had been general rumblings as well as psychological appraisals, and that while he and the Board were deeply reluctant to reach the obvious conclusion (that goalwise we were not a fit), he (and the Board) felt obligated to reach it anyway.

He expressed his fervent wish that things could have worked out differently.

DOES CATHERINE FEEL SORRY FOR YOU?

Yes, I think she does. I think she feels sorry for me because I am not congenitally cheerier. I also get the feeling, unfortunately, that she is a little wary of me—me and my *Weltanschauung*. I think she is troubled by the way I see things, the way I put things. I think she is afraid I will say something unpleasant in one of these little get-togethers, something that will stay with her for way too long. I think she is afraid I might be her Anthony Romero.

ANTHONY ROMERO?

Anthony was a student of mine way back when—an older man. I was teaching Freshman Composition and we were discussing the fine art of building a basic vocabulary. I gave the class an assignment: they could choose any subject, but they were to focus for a page on the use of a varied, natural, and expressive language. I did not forbid the use of a thesaurus, but I cautioned that if one were used, it should be used judiciously—that all synonyms were not created equal. Mr. Romero pretty much ignored this admonition. He wrote about a drive he took into the country—about getting lost, about stopping and looking out "on a field of swaying bovines." Mr. Romero destroyed this bucolic scene for me forever with that phrase. In thirty years I have never been able to look out on a meadow filled with grazing cattle and not first think—ah, a field of swaying bovines. Catherine is afraid I will do something like that to her—make some gloomy comment about the nature of the human condition (about a vast and uncaring infinitude perhaps) that will stay with her for a whole lot longer than she would like.

IT SEEMS IMPORTANT TO CATHERINE THAT YOU NOT BE UPSET ABOUT WHAT HAS HAPPENED.

Catherine has a big heart. She wants to make sure I understand what Fairview is trying to do. She wants me to be more resistant to unhappy thoughts. But, of course, I am not resistant to unhappy thoughts. My tendency is to focus on the dark contingencies. According to the professionals I am a dispositional pessimist, a classic catastrophizer.

AND WHEN YOU LEAVE, YOU WILL BE STAYING FOR A WHILE WITH MICHAEL BERGER?

Yes. Michael and I met several years ago at Greenhurst. He was in a creative-writing class I had been coerced into teaching. He specialized in cryptic stories that oozed metaphysical menace the way a bit-into éclair oozed custard. I liked them. I helped him get funding from a local arts organization to make a short film of *The Visit*, a story of his about a man in a mental institution. I suppose you could say I was sort of Michael's mentor. We became friends.

YOUR RELATIONSHIP IS A LITTLE MORE COMPLICATED THAN THAT ISN'T IT?

I don't know. Probably. I occupy a strange place in his life, some sort of quasi-familial middle-ground—more than a brother figure, but less than a father one. I think we both gave up trying to sort it out a long time ago.

WHAT WERE YOU LIKE AS A PROFESSOR?

Unremarkable, I think. I displayed no charming dottery qualities, no adorable absent-mindedness, no endearing eccentricity (like Gavin Bell, my good friend over in the Music Department). I had a tendency to take an interest only in those who deserved to have an interest taken in them, so I was considered by some to be a cool if not cold person—an elitist, if you will. This perception was tempered somewhat by my attitude toward grading. I was considered—even by Greenhurst's generous standards—to be exceptionally lenient.

WHAT DID YOU TEACH?

My primary field was Postmodern Literature—the sort of literature most people outside of the academic community (and more than a few inside) find virtually impossible not to abhor. I started my career off hopping between community colleges until one day I landed in Portland at Greenhurst. I have been there for almost twenty years. I have—or had—a small office in Millar Hall. It was where I thrived, where I hid from obligatory functions, drank bad coffee, and wrote the articles about X, Y, and Z (mostly mild-mannered attacks on the various conventions of the traditional narrative form) that would eventually secure me tenure.

I specialized in the work of paranoid metafictionists—one in particular. I wrote a book-length introduction to his work that became for a while—a very short while—a standard text in English departments across the country. Emily and I bought a small sailboat with the royalties. We named it *Balderdash*.

I tried on several occasions to interview this man—never with success. It was one of the many things I admired about him—the fact that he was not interested in being a public personality.

3

THIS IS YOUR ROOM?

Yes. It's not bad, all things considered. It reminds me of the one I grew up in—a small laboratory where I experimented with my personality. A bed, a dresser, a triangular-shaped desk wedged into the corner—it was filled with microscopes and model airplanes. On one wall at one time were two dozen pictures of an adolescent English actress, Hayley Mills. Next to the desk was a wicker clothes hamper where I hid bottles of tequila and six-packs of beer .

IS THAT A LETTER?

I have a little time before Michael gets here, so I thought I might write a letter to Alex Hillwood.

WHO IS ALEX HILLWOOD?

Alex is—or was—a colleague. He has a new book out,

a collection of essays titled *The Ideologue*. He sent me a copy. I read it a while ago and was going to send him a note, but then I collapsed on the bathroom floor. I loved the book—well, half of it anyway—and I wanted to thank him.

HALF?

The concluding essay—an extended piece—is what you might call overly comprehensive. It's the story of Alex's torturous conversion, of his finally admitting to himself that his deepest interests lay not in medieval history but in political science. He is too allusive. Too many sentences are sequined—decorated with dropped names and argot-ridden parentheticals. Alex is an obsessive-compulsive—he collects everything: cookie jars, antique tools, opera programs, crime-scene photos. You should see his garage. Some of the paragraphs in this last essay look like that—like his garage.

YOU ACTUALLY APPEAR IN THE BOOK.

I do—in his essay, "Mother Meets Matisse." I appear in an illustrative episode as the abused good samaritan. We were at a conference in New York. Alex had brought Eleanor, his wheelchair-bound mother along. One afternoon we ducked out of a symposium on pedagogical theory and went to the Met—the three of us—to see a Matisse retrospective. It was an extraordinary show. Eleanor was, as always, a handful. Halfway through the thing I thought I'd give Alex a little break and take over the care of mom so he could sit peacefully for a few minutes and contemplate the Odalisques. As they say, no good deed goes unpunished. I wheeled Eleanor and her tangerine-colored hair through four or five galleries before taking her back. She was not happy. She told Alex she would like to go through the galleries again, that for some reason I had refused to take her to the famous kangaroo canvases. At eighty-something Eleanor not only had locomotion issues, but competency ones as well. Somehow, from somewhere, she had gotten the idea that Matisse was famous for painting kangaroos. She greeted my suggestion that she had perhaps confused this painter with some other as the sheerest form of gibberish. She knew the kangaroos were here somewhere—a retrospective of this size was unthinkable without them. It would be like doing Degas without the ballerinas or Monet without the waterlilies. Alex, as the dutiful son, accommodated her. Rather than admit to the possibility of some sort of mystery when no famous kangaroos could be found on this second time through, she simply dismissed the show as fatally flawed.

WHAT WAS YOUR RELATIONSHIP WITH YOUR MOTHER LIKE?

There wasn't much of one. My mother was out of my life completely by the time I was eleven (alcohol, divorce, suicide). She had probably been fading out a long while before that. One of the strongest memories I have of her is from around age nine. I was a Little League baseball pitcher and I needed to practice, but my father was out of town making the world safe for democracy so my mother said she would fill in and catch for me. I threw her a couple of half-speed things to warm her up; then I threw her my fast ball—which was, alas, low and in the dirt. I broke her big toe.

WHO WAS THAT STICKING HIS HEAD IN THE DOOR?

That was Stephen Bishop. He is probably my best friend here. We said our goodbyes last night over at the Kingston where we had dinner and a nice bottle of wine. He was just dropping by to wish me bon voyage. Stephen used to be an airline pilot. He is president of the chess club.

CHESS CLUB?

Yes. This place is ruled by cliques and cabals. There is the chess club, the gardening club, the knitting club, the movie-night club, the travel club, the badminton club—etc., etc., etc. Each has a president and each is involved in some sort of impossibly complex coalition-building—each working in consort with or against the others in the hope of amassing for itself some sort of poorly-defined power. Stephen offered to put in a word for me with management.

STEPHEN LIVES HERE WITH HIS WIFE?

Yes, he is here with his wife, Julie. They are very close. They have been married for forty-two years. Julie's health has been deteriorating lately—more than most, that is. Stephen cannot imagine life without her. It's a secret from the front office (for all sorts of reasons—not the least being legal), but when the time comes, when they are overwhelmed by infirmity and illness, they have decided to take things into their own hands and leave this world together.

STEPHEN HAS A DAUGHTER.

Yes, he does. Christine. She is one of those go-getter business types who knows lots of people and wears her hair pulled back. She is always on her phone, always excusing herself to take this or to take that. She is filled up to her meticulously-plucked eyebrows with insider information. She is very popular with the men in the Investment Club—geezers who for one reason or another don't feel like they have had enough of it all, who are eager to prove they are still players, still smarter than the market. She is personally responsible for bankrupting at least three of them.

WHAT DID HE JUST ASK YOU?

He wants to know if I had heard anything from Emily.

HAVE YOU?

I received a note from her today. She is going to be out of town (or more accurately, out of country) for the next two weeks. She is flying to London with her friend, Allison Kraft.

Allison used to be an auditor for the City Water Bureau, but for the last few years she has been a professional widow. She makes her living talking to women's groups about the ordeal of losing her husband,

Benjamin. She talks about how hard it was, how brave she had to be, how slowly and painfully she came to understand that the world and she were different now. At one point in her most popular presentation she gives a long and gruesome description of the surgery her husband did not survive.

I'm sure they will be discussing me at length—that Emily will mention my proposition, my floating the idea of a reconciliation, of us perhaps living together again. I wish she wouldn't, but I know she will. What can I do? Nothing. There is nothing to be done.

STEPHEN ASKED YOU SOMETHING ABOUT YOUR COAT.

He asked me if it was new. It is. I just picked it up this morning. I bought it at John Helmer's.

HELMER'S?

Yes, it's a small hat-centric haberdashery that has been in business here since 1921. I like their clothes, and I like Mr. Helmer. Once a month he runs a small ad in the *New Yorker* magazine offering 100% wool European Berets. He doesn't really make anything off of these ads—they are just his way of supporting the literary arts and the life of the mind. In my turn—when I get a chance—I support him. When I need a new coat or sweater or umbrella, I buy them from him.

YOU WERE TALKING ABOUT HATS THE OTHER NIGHT.

Yes. Alan Foster showed up in the dining room wearing a dark blue fedora. It was not something that could easily be ignored—which, of course, was the point.

Everyone started talking about it and about hats in general—hats they once had, hats they now had, hats they wish they had had but never did.

AND YOU?

I rarely wear hats. I don't like the way I look in most of them. I have an oddly shaped head that a hat does nothing for, and I'm inclined by nature to keep costuming to a minimum. When I do wear a hat it is for practical reasons—it's either raining hard or very cold. I did once buy a beret—a European one—but not from Mr. Helmer. It was a souvenir. I purchased it at La Samaritaine in Paris. After the trip I didn't have enough money for anything else. I put it on a plaster bust—a desk decoration now relegated to I don't know where.

WHO WAS THAT ON THE PHONE?

That was Gavin Bell, my peculiar friend from Greenhurst. He always calls late. He is having problems with a student by the name of Brianna Haddington—a skinny blonde girl who is obsessed with him. Apparently this sort of thing is not uncommon in the world of classical music. She phones him constantly, writes him, and occasionally breaks into his house. Right now she is very concerned with his health. She read in the newspaper about his recent trip to the hospital. (Gavin is flamboyantly hypochondriacal; he is always making a trip to the hospital.) Her life would be over if anything happened to him. She loves him—loves him more than she loves JFK, and she loves JFK (and his hair) more than anything. She knows Gavin isn't taking care of himself, that his diet consists mostly of pizza, ice cream, and vodka. She wants him to eat better—it is all a matter of antioxidants. She wants him to eat pineapple, red cabbage, and pecans. He found her hiding in his backyard. He chased her off with a garden hose.

IS THAT MICHAEL MAKING HIS GRAND ENTRANCE?

Yes, it is.

FOR SOME REASON I THOUGHT HE WOULD BE TALLER.

Everyone does.

HE'S LATE.

He is a busy young man. He had a meeting this evening with Mark Hamilton. Mark is not a big name himself in the local film community, but he is attached to a big name in the local film community—a production company called something like TranceVision. Mark read about Michael's new project in *Westside Weekly*. It was a piece by an Adam Brown. Adam characterized Michael's new project as "the next big little film from the lauded but still unknown director of one of the last big little films—a finalist for the Oregon Film Prize in the live-action short category: *Richard Introduces Himself.*" (*Richard* is Michael's third film. It is based on a story by Peter Brooks. [See Appendix 1.])

He is late because he had to borrow Geoff Albee's truck. Geoff is one of Michael's neighbors, a musician. He has a truck because he has a band—and apparently a regular obligation to get them from one place to another. Michael is average when it comes to punctuality. I imagine Geoff waylaid him with one of his stories about the hard life of an itinerate guitar player. I'm glad to see he brought a dolly.

WHAT DID HE JUST SAY?

He was complaining. Some of these boxes are pretty heavy. He was wondering why everybody he knows has so many books. I told him it was because he knew so many of the right sort of people.

4

DO WE SENSE A LITTLE TENSION IN THE AIR?

Yes. Between Michael and his inamorata, Jessica. I don't think she is entirely happy about the new living arrangements, about my moving in with them for a while.

SHE DOESN'T LIKE YOU?

No, I don't think it's that she doesn't like me. We have met before on several occasions and almost always had a good time together. I enjoy her quirky take on things, her obsessive obsessiveness. I think the trouble is that she and Michael are having problems at the moment, and she would prefer to be working on them in private.

WHAT SORT OF PROBLEMS ARE THEY HAVING?

I'm not entirely sure. As you might imagine, I have not been made privy to the whole picture. What I have pieced together from comments, vibes, and the general ambiance is that it has something to do with Jessica being jealous, something to do with phone calls from Michael when he was working on *Coffee Girl*—phone calls saying he would be late getting home.

COFFEE GIRL?

Michael's fourth film. It's based on a short story by Phillip Thaw. (See Appendix 2.)

JESSICA SUSPECTS SOMETHING?

She thinks—or thinks she thinks—Michael could be having an affair with Madison Moore, the woman who played the enchanting, cappuccino-sipping, Circe-like lead in the production.

YOUR NEW ROOM IS NICE.

Yes, it is. It's bigger than I expected—and I have a television. But. . . .

BUT WHAT?

The walls are the usual sort of thing—thin. You can hear too much. Mark Twain said he could remember a thing whether it happened or not. Me, I can hear a thing whether it makes a sound or not. An audiologist once told me that I have unique ear canals.

YOU ARE LEAVING EVERYTHING IN BOXES.

Yes. It's a gesture—an ostentatious sign of impermanency. As much as I can, I want my hosts to know that I know this arrangement is only temporary.

WHO IS THAT?

That is Jessica's cat, Pandora. You can see she tries to take a mature, nonserious, species-appropriate attitude toward it, but can't—a fact Michael finds troubling (the blatant expression of surrogacy suggesting certain unresolved progenerative issues). Jessica has hypochondriacal tendencies similar to Gavin's. She is afraid of the cat—the exposure to toxoplasmosis in particular is worrying—but her need for it drives her to ignore the danger.

YOU WENT EXPLORING.

I did. I took a walk around the neighborhood. It has been semi-gentrified. It is not quite what it wants to be yet—which is a cultured version of the sybaritic Pearl—but it is on the way. Lots of people in black with complicated hairdos. I stopped at a small office-supply store for stamps.

WHAT IS MICHAEL DOING?

The second most important piece of equipment in moviemaking is the telephone. Michael has been on his a lot since the *Westside Weekly* article came out. A steady stream of unemployed actors and actresses have been calling to tell him that his new project—*Will There Be Ducks*, based on a story by Kevin Richardson (See Appendix 3)—sounds fascinating and that they would be available to audition for it. He has heard from drama majors, a young man whose mother was in a production of Stoppard's play *Arcadia* two seasons ago, and a woman who played Drug Addict #3 in the local auteur's latest magnum opus.

Some of the applicants have sounded pretty good, and that has been terrible for Michael. He wants the best cast he can get—he knows how important the right person in the right role is for a thing like this—but he has already made certain commitments. I have offered him Faulkner's argument in favor of ruthlessness as an out.

WHICH WAS?

An artist's only responsibility is to his art—everything else goes by the board: honor, decency, happiness, etc., etc., etc. If he has to rob his mother he will not hesitate; *Ode on a Grecian Urn* is worth any number of old ladies.

WHAT ARE YOU HAVING FOR DINNER?

Jessica made spaghetti. She says you can't go wrong with that, and she's right. There are three things that are almost impossible to ruin: scrambled eggs, pumpkin pie, and spaghetti. No matter how bad this or that example, it is almost never inedible—as opposed to say bouillabaisse, which can be a gagging ordeal.

ARE YOU HUNGRY?

Very. I haven't said anything because I didn't want to start right off playing into the stereotype of early-eating old guy. But dinner is, I think, a little behind schedule even for chic, late-eating bon vivants because Jessica was trapped across the hall giving plant advice to her friend Carolyn and was not here to get her special sauce started on time.

Jessica has a green thumb—as evidenced by this apartment.

CAROLYN?

Carolyn Syms. She is a divorced germaphobe. She is constantly scrubbing her apartment. The place gleams and—except for a slight scent of disinfectant—is odorless. It is also frigid—low temperatures inhibit bacterial growth. This, according to Jessica, is one of the things wrong with Carolyn's new dracaena—the place is too cold.

CAROLYN HAS SOME STRANGE DIETARY HABITS.

She does. She is some sort of radical vegetarian. She is always giving Jessica something to take home and try—something involving soy milk and ground flaxseed. She insists that whatever it is tastes better than it sounds—but it never does. Michael thinks she has ulterior motives. He thinks she is part of a vegan cult and is trying to convert Jessica to some sort of new-world macrobioticism one asparagus and ginger root falafel at a time.

Jessica thinks she is just trying to be nice.

WHAT WAS THAT "CONTAMINATED SPINACH" COMMENT ABOUT?

Among Jessica's many sensitivities is a special one to the daily news. She takes it all so hard and is afraid of everything they warn against—drunk drivers, foreclosures, identity theft, police shootings, Republican filibusters, higher electricity rates. I know how she feels. There was a woman at Fairview—Edith Woolf—who refused to answer her door when anybody knocked because she was sure it was someone coming to tell her something horrible. I've gone through long periods when I simply had to ignore what was happening in the world—the Bush years, for instance. I got along (more or less) by pretending the world was what I remembered it being in the 1970s when Nixon resigned.

According to Joe Donlan, the anchor on Channel 8's six o'clock show, the latest threat to our general well-being is contaminated spinach. There has been a nationwide recall of various spinach-related products.

I SEE YOU FOUND YOUR PAJAMAS.

Yes, they were in a box with my dishes. I used them to protect my coffee mug. It's a special one—it's heavy and it fits just so in my hand. I drink everything but wine out of it. I've had it for thirty years.

WHAT IS THIS?

It's a note to myself.

WHAT DOES IT SAY?

Increase daily number of sit-ups.

AND THESE?

Also notes to myself:
Haircut—Tuesday, 12:30.
Re-read Pascal.
Ask Simon for the twenty dollars back.
Check renewal date on passport.
Have eyes tested.
Buy new pair of swimming goggles.

ANY OTHERS?

Yes.

FOR EXAMPLE.

Look into the psychology of whistling—who, where, why.
Find a new shampoo.
Make donation to United Way.

WHAT IS THIS?

Fairview finally forwarded my mail. Two magazines, a clothing catalogue, an oil-change offer, and a postcard from Emily. There are also—as always—a handful of incomprehensible dispatches from my insurers.

WHY DID SHE LEAVE YOU?

I don't think there is a simple answer to that. You are responsible to some degree for who you are and to some degree you're not. I did what I could with the part I was responsible for (or I thought I did anyway)—but that leftover part, the part that I was not responsible for, that just got to be too much for her, which I understand because it got to be too much for me as well. She could leave; I could not.

MICHAEL CALLED.

Yes, he did. He called to say that he would not be making it home for dinner, that he would be late, that he was meeting with Scott Paulson to work on the budget for his *Will There Be Ducks* movie. It looks like he is going to have to shoot the thing in a week. He is worried about not having the time to spend getting crucial scenes right.

Jessica was not happy. There were some heated whispers into the phone.

WHAT DID YOU HAVE FOR DINNER?

Jessica and I had a couple of low-calorie frozen things. Mine was called Fiesta Chicken. The recipe had a Mexican influence. Black beans were involved.

WHAT DID YOU DO AFTER DINNER?

After dinner I went to my room and watched television. I found a movie on channel something-or-other that looked interesting but wasn't—at least not in the way it was intended to be. It was basically an art-house version of a standard May-December romance. A poor, mild-mannered, slightly depressed young lady working in a department store meets and is almost immediately seduced by a single rich man old enough to be her father. I had a hard time going with the flow of the thing, of appreciating its calculatedly "charming" moments because I was constantly distracted by the older actor's creepy plastic face. The actress who played the young girl in the department store was pretty, but not in the emphatic way of most sculpted young movie girls. She had all of her original features—nose, eyes, mouth. The actor who played the older man though— an actor famous in some circles for being a substantive person—he had had something drastic done (several somethings actually) in a pathetically misguided effort to remain handsome and youngish-looking. He was almost unrecognizable—strange in a way that was impossible to satisfactorily analyze.

IT WAS 2 A.M. WHEN YOU HEARD THE FRONT DOOR CLOSE.

Everything wakes me—even with these super-duper foam earplugs. Jessica was awake too. I could hear them arguing in the living room. I couldn't make out what they were saying exactly, but I am pretty sure I heard Michael say the name "Shannon." Shannon was his former girlfriend. I assume he had just accused Jessica of acting like her.

YOU CUT YOURSELF SHAVING THIS MORNING.

I wasn't paying attention—well, not completely. It is a

tiresome task. There must be a better way of spending this time.

MICHAEL LEFT EARLY.

I was sitting down with a bowl of granola when he appeared already dressed. He had a meeting with someone about camera rentals. He wanted to know what I was going to be doing. I told him I had a doctor's appointment and that later I was having lunch with Stephen and Julia.

WHAT IS JESSICA DOING?

She is headed for the grocery store. She wanted to know if there was any particular type of apple I preferred. It struck me as a strange question. I know the choices have multiplied over the years, but for me an apple is still pretty much an apple—unless, of course, you throw caution to the wind and decide to compare it to an orange.

5

WHY THIS VISIT TO THE DOCTOR'S OFFICE?

It is not something I do easily. I'm not especially fond of doctors' offices. I have been having headaches for a while now. I am not inclined to see brain tumors at every turn. I was, however, convinced by Catherine Cain—given my recent history—that an exam was warranted.

DR. NESBITT.

I got his name from Patrick Warner, an acquaintance at Fairview. He has an excellent reputation, Dr. Nesbitt— you just have to ignore the fact that for some reason he thought it would be a good idea to do something interesting with his mustache.

THEY TOOK XRAYS.

They did. And, of course, they insisted on showing me.

Is there anything more completely disorienting than a picture of your brain? (Where in the fat folds of that gray loaf was my memory of Emily in her cashmere sweater; my ability to add, subtract, and divide; my opinion of *Crime and Punishment*?) I was so focused on appearing normal when they showed these to me, on looking interested, blasé—anything but what I was, which was horrified—that I could barely hear a word of the good doctor's good news—no tumor, no surgery, no iffy odds. There it was, in black and white—my brain, the birthplace of my happiness, my worry, my very awareness of happiness and worry. How could I look on that and not be turned to stone.

WHAT WAS JESSICA DOING WHEN YOU GOT HOME?

Those are breathing exercises. I'm not sure where she got them—probably a self-help book (there are dozens laying around). She might have gotten them from a shrink. I haven't asked, but there is something about the language she uses ("conflicted," "empowered," "codependent") and the flex of her general anxiety that makes me think she is seeing one. These breathing exercises are supposed to calm her down. Carolyn suggested she try yoga.

SHE SAYS YOU ARE PALE.

She thinks I need more sun. She preaches its virtues as a source of Vitamin D a little stridently, I think. It is in part a rationalization of her own behavior—of her flagrant disregard of current injunctions. She thinks she looks ill if she isn't at least a little bit tan.

HOW WAS LUNCH WITH STEPHEN AND JULIA?

Lovely. As I was getting dressed for the adventure I could hear Emily's quiet counsel. My taste in clothes runs to the utilitarian and mute—that is, practical stuff that steadfastly refuses to make a statement. My tendency is to wear old, comfortable things—things that may or may not be wrinkled, things that may or may not be slightly faded, things that may or may not be fraying a bit at the cuffs and collar. Emily, who is fastidious in these matters (an inheritance from her preternaturally fastidious mother), insists there are standards. I agree. I believe in standards. What we disagreed about was what they were and when they applied.

I remember a note I once wrote to an author. I had seen him on stage at a Portland Arts and Lectures event. He appeared there with three other nascent eminences as part of a panel discussion on what it meant to be a young writer in America these days. The event was held in one of those large, elaborately refurbished downtown movie palaces. Everyone on stage and in the audience was, to some degree, gussied-up for the occasion—everyone except this particular young man, that is. He arrived wearing a pair of big blond work boots, ratty jeans, and some sort of long-sleeved, waffle-weave undershirt. He looked like a down-on-his-luck logger.

There was a tripartite reading, a tripartite colloquy (with moderator), and a tripartite question-and-answer session. Something this young man said about his nervousness and the peculiarity of the affair made me think of an old Kurt Vonnegut anecdote. (Vonnegut was nervous about giving a speech. He didn't think it was any good. He mentioned this *sotto voce* to the dignitary sitting on the dais beside him, and this man told him by way of reassurance that he, KV, shouldn't worry about it. Nobody really cared anything about what he had to say—they were just there because they wanted to see if he was an honest man.) When I got home I wrote the young writer a note passing this little story on. I introduced myself and explained that I had just seen him "flamboyantly underdressed" at the Arts and Lectures do-da in Portland. A few weeks later the young man wrote back. He used a small thank-you card (EXPRESSIONS from Hallmark). He said he understood Vonnegut's unease: "These writerly forums are *a priori* impossible to be honest at." In a postscript he replied good-naturedly to my comment about his appearance. He wrote, "I was not underdressed. The lady said casual—the other 3 were overdressed."

WAS THAT ANOTHER LATE-NIGHT CALL FROM GAVIN?

It was. He wanted to talk about a television show he had just seen, a hospital drama from the 1980s. One of the subplots in this particular episode involved a mental patient who thought he and the hospital staff were characters from *The Mary Tyler Moore Show*— the grumpy boss, the slubby co-worker, the gaudy neighbor. Not only were roles reversed and transposed, so too were the real-life actors and actresses. People who were familiar as characters on one show turned up in this one as doppelgangers and comic counterparts. Gavin thought the various layers of ironic self-reference would be interesting to me as a professor of postmodernism, and he was right—though I should admit I got a little lost in his less-than-linear synopsis. It was obviously the sort of thing that really had to be seen to be fully appreciated.

What caught Gavin's interest (Gavin who is not a professor of postmodernism) was the *Mary Tyler Moore* angle. He is a long-time devotee of that show. He knows it inside and out and has bored me silly with detailed reviews on innumerable occasions. This show is one of Emily's favorites too, and though she has her problems with Gavin and his extravagant personality, she respects his intelligence and thinks this shared enthusiasm reflects well on her.

WHEN WAS THE LAST TIME YOU ACTUALLY SAW EMILY?

I'm not exactly sure. I remember she had a new haircut. Her friend, Allison, was giving her grooming tips. She told Emily a slightly shorter haircut would be better. What sort of advice is that? For every time a slightly shorter haircut is the answer, there are ten times when it isn't. It was foolish for Emily to ignore the odds. Of course, everyone thinks it's "darling."

YOU LOOK TIRED.

Sleeping fitfully as usual. Warm my cares with a cavalcade of worst-case scenarios.

YOU STAYED UP LATE READING.

I did. I re-read one of my old favorites last night—a novel once described in passing as "a genre unto itself." It saddens me to realize how alone I am these days in my admiration for this sort of thing.

WHAT WAS JESSICA TALKING ABOUT THIS MORNING?

The newest news—a suspected kidnapping. Her general fearfulness reminds me of my own and of Emily's.

Me, I am afraid of all sorts of things: I'm afraid I will be late; I'm afraid the refrigerator will stop working; I'm afraid the car will stop working; I'm afraid the television will stop working; I'm afraid I will have to have a filling replaced or a tooth pulled; I'm afraid the price of my favorite wine will go up; I'm afraid the bookstore on the corner will close; I'm afraid the waitress at my pizza place will leave; I'm afraid I will make a wrong turn, get lost, and, as a consequence, have a part of my life—a part I will never get back—eaten by anxiety and stress.

Emily—well, Emily is always hearing strange noises, smelling strange smells, sensing something going wrong somewhere—something bad happening upstairs when we are down and downstairs when we are up.

The last time I saw her (with her new short hairdo), she was carrying a copy of Simon Gray's *Smoking Diaries*. I had to smile. She always carries a copy of something so if we are in an accident and have to go to the hospital, she—who always emerges miraculously unscathed in these little tragedies—will have something to read while she waits for word of my condition.

YOU HAD A SPLINTER.

I did. I spent forever on it this afternoon—forever locating it, forever extracting it, forever bandaging myself up.

MICHAEL IS HAVING A SMALL DINNER PARTY.

He is trying to raise money for *Ducks*. He and Jessica have invited two other couples—Cheryl Hayes and her boyfriend, Roger; Maria Beech and her boyfriend, Donald. The plan is for them to talk Maria's boyfriend, Donald, into investing. He comes from money. If he decides to take the plunge there just might be a small part in the thing for Maria. She could be "Kathy" (aka, girl #1) at the office.

HASN'T ROGER WORKED WITH MICHAEL BEFORE?

Roger Gross, Cheryl's boyfriend, is a film-school dropout. He is Michael's assistant—his gofer. He takes care of the nuts-and-bolts stuff—equipment rentals, insurance, caterers, that sort of thing. Michael showed me a copy of the budget for *Richard Introduces Himself*. It was boggling all the things you needed to think about and pay for.

MICHAEL IS DESPERATE TO GET STARTED ON *DUCKS*.

It has been months since he has worked on something of his own. He just finished making a commercial. It was for a local car dealer—a man who insisted on using a mascot. The idea was you should buy a Chevy from this guy because—well, he had an Australian accent and a Wallaby. Michael wants to be distracted from this sort of stuff—he wants to get into the nightmare of his next production. Money from Donald (Maria's boyfriend) is only step six or seven in an I-don't-know-how-many-steps process. Wonders remain to be imagined.

WHAT IS THAT? ARE YOU BACK WORKING ON THE MEMOIR?

Assisted Living—yes. I thought I would spend a page or two on old girlfriends.

ANY NAMES?

There was early on—when I was almost in my teens—Susan Nichols. I remember very little except for the preposterousness of the obsession, the savageness of the rejection, and the totality of the humiliation.

Then there was Annette something-or-other. She was Italian. She owned an aquarium and lived with her mother in a not-very-nice apartment complex just off of 44th and Thompson. As I recall, she left me for an eighteen-year-old with a nice car and an interest in marine biology.

WHO DID YOU HAVE DINNER WITH LAST NIGHT?

I had dinner last night with Lawrence Chapman. He used to be a professor—a Carlyle expert. He wrote two impenetrable books on the great man—one on his relationship to the Scottish Enlightenment, the other on his theory of history. Lawrence started writing detective novels as a sort of cognitive counterbalance to his immersion in the pyrotechnical quagmire of *Past and Present*. His sleuth, a man named James Granite, is an ex-cop with a drinking problem who plies his trade in a small New England town where, it seems, a surprising number of people are being killed by psychopaths. Lawrence quit the professing business when he sold his Granite books to television.

We talked for a bit about my situation, but mostly we talked about Rebecca, Lawrence's wayward wife. Two months ago she came home from her psychiatrist's office with a new prescription; she hasn't been the same since. Lawrence is wary of embracing this new entity (this pharmaceutically-improved Rebecca) because if he does and she suddenly disappears—which is entirely possible for just as Rebecca had once been against pill-popping and changed her mind, she could change it back again, be against it again, and stop—he will have left himself open to a charge of philandering, of having preferred this "other woman," this malleable, less problematic woman, all along, etc., etc., etc.

YOU WANTED TO ADD SOMETHING?

I have to mention Lawrence's eyebrows. They are huge like hawk wings. They flap up and down when he talks. They distract you. They make it impossible to accurately interpret a plethora of micro-expressions.

AND?

One thing in particular Lawrence wanted to talk about—eyebrows flapping—was a pie Rebecca had bought him.

It was from Jacaiva's. Lawrence loves Jacaiva pies, but Rebecca had bought blueberry. Lawrence is allergic to blueberries. Rebecca knows this. Once in their early days together she had given him a muffin with blueberries in it. He spent the night in the hospital. Was the new and improved Rebecca trying to do him harm?

WHAT IS THAT NOISE?

Boys bouncing balls. Apparently at the age of nine this is something that can be done for hours.

6

WHAT WERE YOU SAYING TO JESSICA?

I couldn't help but comment on her bowl of cereal this morning—it was huge, a mix of several different kinds with granola and bananas tossed in. She is stuffing herself because she isn't going to be having much of a lunch. She is meeting Carolyn. (Likely subject of conversation: Teresa Knight's new nose job.)

DID YOU HEAR SOMETHING FROM EMILY?

Yes, I just got a postcard. She is not coming home with Allison. She is flying on to France to visit our son Richard and his innumerable complaints.

MICHAEL SEEMS TO HAVE SOME CASTING ISSUES.

He wants Jay Parkhouse to play Tim Cummings (Steven's obviously-troubled work buddy), but Jay isn't interested. It's not something he wants to do. Michael thinks Jay would be perfect, that he has the right everything for the part—the right bone structure, the right back story, the right bearing. He thinks without him the movie will be marred.

WHAT ARE YOU LOOKING FOR?

I'm looking for a photo I have of Emily as a child. She is standing in a driveway, hand-in-paw with a six-foot Easter Bunny. So far no luck.

WHERE DID YOU MEET RACHEL?

There are four apartments on each floor of this building—Jessica and Michael are here; across the hall is Carolyn; down the hall on the same side as Carolyn is Rachel; and across from her on the same side as Jessica and Michael are the Osborns. In the middle of each floor, across from the elevator, is a shared laundry room. That is where I met Rachel. Jessica warned me about her. She habitually leaves things in the washing machine making it impossible for others to use. If I found stuff left in the washing machine I was supposed to take it out and pile it on the laundry table—which is what I was doing when Rachel walked in. She thought I was a pervert—some old man monkeying with her underwear. I explained myself as best I could.

DESCRIBE HER.

Tall, thin—the sort of woman who rinses her hair with lemon juice. She has a crush on her chiropractor.

WHAT IS EVERYONE UPSET ABOUT?

A parking ticket. Michael missed the meter by ten minutes.

YOU VISITED SUNCREST TODAY.

It was recommended by a friend of Stephen Bishop as being the next best thing to Fairview. I don't know about it being the next best thing, but it is certainly reminiscent. Set back a bit on an unexpected hill rise, it looks like an older, slightly less prosperous version of the place.

A woman named Adel—one of a cadre of volunteer emissaries—showed me around. She was just back from visiting her son, a large-animal vet in Phoenix, Arizona. I haven't been away from Fairview long, but it seems I have already regained a sense of myself that suggests I am not the sort of person who belongs in a place like this. It worries me, the re-emergence of this pre-heart-attack personality. It is going to make reconciling myself to the realities of the situation much more difficult.

YOU DIDN'T CARE FOR THE PLACE?

No. Adel did her gracious best to beguile me, but alas to no avail. I didn't care for the acoustics. (Too much easy-care linoleum.) Also, there were olfactory issues—distant scents of not-so-distant scents obscured. Suncrest would be fine if there was nothing else, but there has to be something else, doesn't there?

WHAT WAS THAT ABOUT CAROLYN'S BROTHER?

I just found out he is a priest. It came as sort of a shock to me. I didn't know people actually became priests anymore. It seems sort of like becoming a blacksmith.

YOU FINALY MET KEVIN RICHARDSON.

Yes, the young man who wrote *Will There Be Ducks*. Michael brought him over to the apartment last night. He also wrote (or is still in the process of writing) the screenplay.

HAVE YOU READ IT?

Yes. It is a sort of figurative (and literal) stalker story. It opens with a five-year-old's stream-of-consciousness reverie. He is in a station wagon with his mother. She is talking non-stop about the miraculous new life they are headed for in Seattle. As he watches the highway fly by he thinks about the life he is leaving behind—a life where he and his friends used to chase each other for no reason, where they used to throw oranges at the ghosts in his grandmother's garage. He is wondering about the new life—the one he is heading toward. Was there going to be anything to do in it, anyone to do it with? Would it be a life of sitting in the kitchen watching his mother cry? Would there be ducks where they were going? Would there be a boat?

The reference is reprised at the end of the story.

AND?

I have my own theories, of course. I know better than to ask for an interpretation. I would say its general concerns are with something other than simple story.

YOU AND MICHAEL HAD A LITTLE DEBATE ABOUT CINEMATIC TACTICS.

We did. He thinks Kevin's opening scenes are a little too "on the nose." He would prefer a little trickery and obfuscation—a strategic delay of the audience's comprehension. He finds my reluctance to embrace this approach amusing.

MICHAEL SEEMS A LITTLE TENSE.

He wants *Ducks* to be good. One of the things at stake for him is the chance to move on—to make the next film. If *Ducks* is good, there will be favorable attention. Favorable attention means investors, and investors mean a chance at another outing.

WHO IS THAT?

Brandon Weeks. He is sitting in on the script conference today. He is a friend of Michael's, and he is making his own movie—a movie about Michael making *his* movie. Adding one more loop to the regressive loopty loo, he has hired a guy named Tony Farnetti. He is going to be filming Brandon—Brandon filming Michael. I haven't met him yet, Tony.

WHAT WERE YOU TALKING TO KEVIN ABOUT?

I was talking with him about his brief sojourn in a mental institution. He said it was illuminating, that half of the inmates were just writers looking for material.

WORK ON *ASSISTED LIVING*?

Yes. There are milestones in one's life—getting your driver's license, losing your virginity, having a child. For me there was getting my first answering machine and screening my first call. I am going to write a page or so on that.

BUT?

But I think I'll skip the trenchant comedy of my high-school years—forgo the disgraceful encounter with trigonometry and my introduction to alcohol.

WHAT WAS THIS PARTY YOU WENT TO?

I went to a party at the Carters last night—mostly in the hope of being able to report it to Emily. I want her to know I am a new (or partly new) man, that while not exactly gregarious, I am—post-heart-attack—gregariouser. It was the usual sort of thing—drinks and lots of talk about how beautiful the house is. Also lots of talk about health care, taxes, and estate planning. And Gordon Kennedy—who killed himself two weeks ago. (Unhappy widower, he drove his car into a concrete bridge abutment.)

GESUNDHEIT.

I'm allergic to whatever it is that blooms earliest in spring. My eyes start to itch. My nose runs. I can't sleep. I take over-the-counter antihistamines, but I don't like them very much. They do what they're supposed to do with regard to my symptoms, but they make me feel funny—which means from the end of February to the middle of April I am not quite myself. The sad thing is, during this time I am not quite anybody else either.

YOU SEEM A LITTLE SUBDUED.

When you hit your sixties everything starts to seem like a cliché—including sixty-year-olds who think everything seems like a cliché.

WHAT IF YOU HAD IT ALL TO DO OVER AGAIN?

If I actually had it to do over again, I suppose I would have learned how to ice skate and to play the piano.

7

YOU RAN INTO RACHEL AGAIN.

I did. She says she thinks it's Mr. Osborn who is playing with her underwear, not me. I ask her if she is so worried about people touching her things, why does she keep leaving them down here. She says she has a busy life, and she forgets—like this time she was on the telephone with her sister in San Diego. Apparently she is quitting another job.

DOES JESSICA ALWAYS TALK TO THE TELEVISION?

Only when she is watching the news. This afternoon she told one reporter that she didn't believe a word he said about a certain missing seventeen-year-old. She had seen a picture of the girl and heard some of the sordid details of her troubled life, and she couldn't believe she was the only person in Portland who could see something horrible like this coming.

She blasted another reporter's suggestion to

everyone in an Aloha neighborhood that they keep an eye on their car because there had been a "rash" of break-ins. Thanks, Stephanie—we all know about the break-ins. It never would have occurred to us to keep an eye on our cars if we hadn't just happened to be watching the news and gotten your sage advice.

WHAT WAS JESSICA JUST ASKING YOU ABOUT?

Carolyn has a new boyfriend, John—a recovering alcoholic. He is just out of rehab and looks a little rickety. Jessica doesn't understand the attraction. She wants to know if I have any ideas. I told her she was asking the wrong person. While Carolyn likes to talk to Jessica about this guy, she has not been particularly eager to introduce them because Jessica is younger and prettier and Carolyn is feeling fragile at the moment and doesn't think she could stand watching him try not to notice.

According to Jessica, Carolyn has always had appalling taste in men. She attributes this in large part to Carolyn growing up with an insane mother. (Jessica is always ready to give a break to someone with an insane mother.) Mrs. Syms (Carolyn's mother) was a strange kind of crazy—sort of like Lee Harvey Oswald's mother. She talked a level-headed sort of nonsense. She was batshit, but she didn't seem like it—not at first anyway.

WAS THAT GAVIN ON THE PHONE?

Yes, it was. He is very excited. He has worked out some sort of arrangement with Greenhurst that means no more lecturing. There will be the occasional private student, but lecturing is over. He is free to work almost exclusively on his recordings and his encyclopedia. He ended the call with a list of his current ailments. They included high blood pressure, skeletal misalignment, kidney pain, and tightened throat.

WHAT IS THIS ABOUT BEETLES?

Right now Jessica is obsessed with the threat of a box-elder beetle infestation. The apartment building next to the one next to this one has them, and she is certain they are coming. She has left several messages with the company that manages the building for the owner (who apparently lives in Hong Kong), but she has not heard anything back.

WHAT WAS BRANDON TALKING ABOUT?

Brandon showed up this morning with a long and very boring story about Chris Eaton (a crew member) having his bicycle stolen.

YOU VISITED THE SET OF *DUCKS* LAST NIGHT.

Yes, I did—and I got pressed into service as an unpaid extra. They were doing the Steven-exits-the-bar scene. I played (quite convincingly, I think) the older, put-upon guy who Steven bumps into on his drunken way out to the parking lot.

Kill your darlings—that was someone's advice to writers. Maybe someone should give the same advice to filmmakers. Michael has a few darlings in this project, but none more darling than the scene where Steven's car hits a light pole, and the lantern—a thing roughly the size and shape of a rural mailbox—comes crashing down into the windshield. A clearly symbolic moment that is referred to time and time again in the story, Michael wants to stylize it. He wants to capture it just so. It's a tricky thing for lots of reasons—not the least of which is that the car (the "sad little rattletrap") is borrowed, and reparations for any damage done to it will be coming out of an already too-taxed budget.

YOU SAT WITH BRANDON FOR AN INTERVIEW ABOUT MICHAEL AND THE MOVIE.

I did. Brandon saw some footage of the other night. He complimented me on my portrayal of the put-upon old-guy. I had to admit it wasn't really much of a stretch.

He wanted my take on what Michael was trying to do with this film. I told him I wasn't sure I knew—and I wasn't sure Michael knew. I told him that so far as I could tell—elaborate theoretical proclamations aside—he was (with a bit of do-da here, a bit of do-da there, and some formal shenanigans over yonder) simply trying to find a different way of doing things, that he was not trying to move his work into the mainstream (which was of no interest to him at all), but out of the pedigreed adventurist's ghetto of mutual regard that was originally his home.

WHAT ELSE DID HE ASK YOU?

He asked about Michael's reaction to the general lack

of interest in *Andrew* (Michael's third effort), to the speculation that this signaled it was over for him—that it was back to car commercials. I told him I couldn't say, but I had the impression that Michael was pretty much immune to that sort of stuff.

AND?

He asked about Michael's reviews. I told him from what I had seen, Michael was getting lumped in with the wrong crowd pretty regularly. I did not think he had an argument with virtuosity or contrivance, that his discomfort was with certain traditional methods, not with coherence—although at times it could seem so.

YOU LOOK ANNOYED.

The wind today ruined my last good umbrella—the black, telescoping one with the hooked handle. I can't replace it because for some reason the people who used to make it have stopped making it, and, so far as I can tell, nobody else has started. I'm going to have to move to a different style, one with a straight, knob-like handle. I can tell you right now that I am never going to like it as much.

WHERE IS JESSICA?

Jessica is out with her friend Mia. She wanted to talk to her about this Madison Moore—get it off her chest. She thinks there is something going on with Michael and her. (Madison—from *Coffee Girl*—is playing Miss Stands-Out-In-A-Crowd [aka Miss Watches-Her-Weight, and/

or Miss Cleaner-Than-Thou], the young lady who Steven stalks briefly at the end of *Ducks*.) She—this Madison—has apparently told Michael that he looks like someone famous, but she can't quite think of who. Why would she do that? He doesn't look like anybody famous; he looks like Michael. Jessica has watched her talking to him on the set. She has watched Madison slide her delicate hand across his shoulder. (Michael will feel that down to his toes. He is sensitive to being touched). How long before he sleeps with her? Maybe he has slept with her already.

YOU WERE IMAGINING DINNER WITH EMILY.

I was. At Lazlo's. We were talking. She has thought about it, about our getting back together, about my moving in, but she doesn't think it will work. I, of course, accept this.

Emily is a fairly popular woman at the moment. There are two men competing for her attention—even though she has encouraged neither. Man #1 is president of their condo board and, consequently, the slightly more interesting of the two. Unfortunately, he is technically still married—although he and his wife have not lived together for a couple of years (she having taken up with Jesus). He is leading the condo association into a complex and protracted legal battle with the builder for construction defects. Man #2 is the president of nothing. He is sensitive, quiet, kind, and low-key. A relationship with #1—if Emily were interested—would be too complicated, and with #2 not complicated enough. Each has qualities I don't have, which Emily occasionally thinks would be nice: #1, a loud voice and a comfortableness in the world; #2, a mysterious, contented outdoorsyness. Why won't she tell me if either of these Prince Charmings knows about the other?

WHAT ARE YOU SMILING ABOUT?

I overheard a joking conversation about a possible camping trip. I like being in the woods for about an hour. I used to like being in them longer, but something has happened to me. Jessica is a little frightened of them; she thinks they're creepy. She made Michael promise never to take her into them unless it was absolutely necessary. I suspect she imagines them to be filled with one or another sort of goblin. I find them soothing and significant—a place to find perspective. But I am only interested in being soothed or placed into a larger context for a short time. I get bored even though I know I'm not supposed to. After I've breathed the air, listened to the sound of nothing, and had lunch on a flat rock, I'm done.

YOU JUST GOT OFF THE PHONE WITH LAWRENCE.

I did. I told him about my imaginary rendezvous with Emily—about her saying "no" to the proposed living arrangement. He told me about a place called Winterbrook and gave me the name of a friend of his who has been there for a couple of years now—Nathan Wilsey. He told me I should contact him. In parting, I asked about his new and improved Rebecca. He says there has been no change. He told me she has started giving him theatrical kisses on the forehead. They are meant to be playful and affectionate, but he can't bring himself to respond.

WHAT DID YOU SAY ABOUT TUNA FISH?

I'm giving up tuna fish sandwiches. I don't like the way they make the room smell.

WHAT ARE YOU DOING?

I am back writing *Assisted Living*. My subject: a long-ago, too-early encounter with the idea of "infinity."

There is probably a perfect age to begin contemplating something like endlessness, but I have no idea what it is. I'm pretty sure it isn't eight—at least it wasn't for me. As a complex piece of inspired imagining, it wasn't, of course, something I just came up with myself. It was handed to me by my grandfather—a biology professor who at one point in his life looked very much like the English philosopher Bertrand Russell (same hair, same rodential muzzle, same beaky nose). He was always giving me stuff he shouldn't—a pocket knife, sips from his martini, a nightmare-inducing story about flesh-eating bacteria. I remember laying out in the backyard all night staring up at the sky trying to comprehend the existence of something with no beginning and no end. I would think to the left for a while toward the beginning until I got completely lost, then start to the right toward the end. I could think in that direction longer, but in the end (or should I say "toward the end") the result was the same: confusion and a profound disorientation. I injured myself. I became in some way, I think, prematurely peculiar.

WHAT IS THAT WORD?

"Phantasm." My handwriting has never been very good. It lacks everything good handwriting should have: balance, beauty, clarity, grace. If it were a voice, it would be Donald Duck's. At its worst, it is simply illegible—the graphological equivalent of a lost breakfast. The horrors of one's handwriting are accentuated, I have noticed, by what I think of as writing's cruelest invention—the fine-point pen. It emphasizes the scraggly and chaotic qualities of one's script. I blame this instrument on accountants and their intricately crosshatched ledger sheets—as they have proliferated, so too have these pens. They are everywhere: fine, extra-fine, extra-extra-fine—pens that could only be of interest to an acupuncturist.

WHERE WERE YOU?

I went for a walk. Scolded by a crow.

8

WHOSE APARTMENT IS THIS?

Rick Wolfe's. Michael is using it to shoot the bathroom scene of *Ducks*. He is not happy. This is the third location so far that has not really been what it needed to be, where they have had to improvise and make do. This bathroom is too big, too bright, too expensive-looking. They had to shrink it, darken it, cheapen it, austere-ize it—which they did, but the results are still not what Michael hoped. It lacks authenticity. The shooting schedule is tight—there is no time to look for something else like a better set, a different shot.

WOULD YOU DESCRIBE THE SCENE?

It is the morning after Steven's accident. The alarm clock goes off. He is in the bathroom trying to shave around all of his cuts and stitches. He can barely recognize himself with all that swelling. He stares at the mess in front of him and remembers his first fistfight.

It was with a boy named Alan Peacock. He has no idea what it was about. He does, however, remember wishing it had been with someone else, someone more popular, someone more coordinated, someone whose defeat would have bequeathed him greater honor. Steven turns on a small, unimpressive little radio. He listens to NPR, to a story about a cinnamon bun that looked like Mother Teresa. It had been stolen from a coffeehouse in Nashville.

WHO IS JESSICA ON THE PHONE WITH?

She has a sister, Cynthia—one year older. They are friends, but they were in constant competition throughout childhood, each sensitive to the other getting some sort of preferred treatment—usually sister Cynthia because she was older (the bigger bedroom, the furrier stuffed panda), but sometimes Jessica because she was younger (the first piece of pie at Thanksgiving). Neither of them bought this older/younger argument—they thought it was because Mom or Dad liked the other best and it just wasn't fair—everybody was against them. This has carried over into the present—Jessica's sensitivity. She is convinced Michael likes Madison (Miss Stands-Out-In-A-Crowd) more than he likes her. She repeats the story to Cynthia—the one she told Mia—about the young lady putting her hand on Michael's shoulder.

YOU WERE TALKING TO BRANDON AGAIN.

Yes. It was a follow-up to the interview. He wanted some background, a synopsis of my aesthetic preferences. I told him basically I don't like music that is decibel-dependent, painting that is concept-dependent, novels that are dialogue-dependent, or movies that are spectacle-dependent.

CAN HE USE THAT?

I have no idea.

WHO WAS IT THAT YOU JUST CALLED?

I was talking with Allison. She said Emily would not be back next week, but maybe the week after. She said Emily was considering a consulting job. Said she would be giving speeches to still-active real-estate agents. Some travel would be involved.

If E decides to do it, I know she will do it wonderfully. It is something I have always admired about her—the ability to commit fully to whatever task. Me—I'm never fully anywhere. Some part of me is always off somewhere else.

YOU TOOK A TRIP OUT TO WINTERBROOK.

I did. I went out to have a look around and to meet Nathan Wilsey, the man Lawrence told me about.

WHAT DID YOU THINK?

I liked the place. It is less institutional than most—lots of brick and stone, lots of odd angles.

Wilsey is a character—he has one of those eccentric, unkempt, statement-making beards. You get the feeling he is one of those people who has lived much of his life as it should be lived (as a poet in touch with nature) while you were living yours in quiet desperation trying to make some sort of expensive electronic gizmo work the way it was advertised to. He was locked up once for sending threatening letters to the head of the local cable company, his congressman, and the attorney who represented his wife in divorce proceedings. He was confined for several months—diagnosed as a danger to himself and others. A reporter named Burgess wrote a story about him. He presented Nathan as a heroic anti-modernist imprisoned by capitalism's craven henchmen.

We took a nice long walk along the river, Nathan wheezing pretty much all the way. It was emphysema that brought him to Winterbrook. I told him I was working on a book and required time to myself. He said it was available here—all I had to do was fend off an initial barrage of invitations to participate.

He wanted to know what the book is about. I told him it was about how things are with me right now and how they were from time to time in the past. He didn't seem particularly curious, but I gave him an example anyway—mostly because I wanted to hear how some of these things sounded said out loud. I told him about inadvertently poisoning the Thompson girl when I was ten with a jar of unidentified fumes—something I had captured from a mix of swimming pool chemicals, acid, and chlorine.

YOU ARE WORRIED ABOUT JESSICA?

I get the feeling she thinks I am a bad influence in

some ways, that she thinks I somehow give Michael license to indulge the morbid side of his personality—a side Jessica doesn't like and is afraid will one day overwhelm him. She is probably right.

BACK WORKING ON *ASSISTED LIVING?*

Yes. It is August, and I am staying at the beach with my parents and the Caldwells. The Caldwells, for reasons not entirely clear to me, seem genuinely fond of my mother and father. They have, in a sense, adopted them. No one I know would call the Caldwells "rich" because that would be gauche—but they are "rich." They have a huge house in the city and this more-than-ample one here. The house in the city has pillars out front and is at the end of a long, curved drive that is lined with small, symmetrical hedges linked like so many sausages. This one, the beach house, is covered with white clapboards. It is cornily Cape Coddish. Each summer the Caldwells invite my parents to visit; each summer my parents invite me. The Caldwells are older; their children are long gone. Me—I am too young to have flown. Here at the beach it is my lot in life to be superfluous—and superfluous I am, with a vengeance.

YOU TALKED WITH LAWRENCE LAST NIGHT.

I told him that after conversations with people from three other places, I had decided on Winterbrook—unless, of course, I heard something unexpected and definitive from Emily the Enigmatic. As I have said, the place doesn't look nearly as institutional as some. The rooms are a nice size and intelligently laid out.

They have outstanding medical facilities (in case I fall over again), and I have had a confirmation from two administrators about what Nathan said—that they are a hands-off organization unless you ask for hands-on.

WHAT IS THAT?

My new driver's license. The photo is shocking. They're always bad, but this one is the baddest ever. I look like my father's grandfather. I've got two chins, a funny neck, and the flash has turned my mustache completely white.

IT'S NICE OUT.

As a rule I have a tendency to be in favor of moderation—except when it comes to temperature. Sixty degrees, like it is today, is roughly speaking the climatic equivalent of the middle way. It's bland—like modesty. It's probably my least favorite temperature. It's neither stimulating nor stupefying. It's blah—like chicken broth.

YOU HAD A DREAM LAST NIGHT.

I did. In it my name was James. It was like I was a character in a short story, a father—one of those who is a little more fatherly than the average father you find in everyday life; one of those with a fatherly haircut and a cleft chin; one of those who wakes up in the middle of the night with his pajamas soaked in sweat, his heart pounding, terrified his daughter has been kidnapped by the worst sort of person he can imagine—someone with no known address, someone stalky and hairy and smelly, someone with stubby fingers and hideous intentions. One of those fathers who jumps up and rushes across the hall to check on his little girl. There she is. Her name is Lindsay. She is eight and beautiful—a daughter made up of the best parts of other people's daughters (Mark's, Bill's, David's)—the daughter I would have if I could have the daughter I wanted. There she is, curled up like a cat, asleep under her favorite fuzzy blanket.

ASSISTED LIVING AGAIN?

Yes. Notes about a long-ago visit to New York—about taking the train out to Flushing to watch the Mets play the Cards. I remember in the middle of the pre-game announcements that it was suggested we report any incidences of "antisocial behavior" to the nearest usher. That caught me by surprise. Being antisocial isn't something I expected a New Yorker to notice, let alone object to.

Benchley once wrote a piece titled "So You're Going To New York" telling tourists that when it came to visiting points of interest in the city, they were as likely as not to find them torn down or closed. He wrote that in 1929.

In addition to the library and Bryant Park, this is a partial list of things I remember finding closed in the course of a four-day visit:

Backstage on Broadway Tour
Leo Castelli Gallery
Lutece's
Elaine's for lunch

The Rose Room at the Algonquin
Lou Singer's Ethnic Tour of Brooklyn
Angelina's

67

YOU BOUGHT A BOOK.

I bought another book about mathematics, and I can't say why exactly. I don't have a mathematical bone in my body, but there is something about these strange arguments I find irresistible. It feels like a way for me to run my thumb along the edge of something.

ARE YOU FINDING THESE RECOLLECTIONS HELPFUL?

I think part of me is expecting to be rejuvenated by these recollections. So far that part has been disappointed.

9

IS JESSICA TRYING TO MAKE NEW FRIENDS?

Yes—which explains Ashley, who I have met several times now. She is always wanting to share some story about someone in her family who did something or other and I have to sit here listening and looking deeply interested when all I really want is for her to stop talking to me and go away so I can get back to doing whatever it is I was doing before she stopped by. I am always afraid that somehow it's obvious that this is what I want, that whoever it is I'm talking to knows what I'm thinking, that it's written all over my face, given away by all sorts of involuntary flickers and twitches, so I try extra hard to have a sincerely engaged expression because as much as I want her to go away, I don't want to hurt her feelings.

WHO IS COLIN WAKE?

The man who is supposed to take my picture for the

Greenhurst Alumni Magazine. He is a veteran of the fashion scene. He has long gray hair—like a lion's mane—which he combs back and goops in place so that it looks as if he has been caught, stop-action, staring into a gale-force wind. He has a signature style that trades heavily on the inherent drama of the black-and-white photo. He wants to make me look if not famous, at least significant—like someone from an earlier, more serious time. He posed me just off to the left of an ornately framed window, my chin up, my focus on posterity.

I don't like the finished product at all. I look grave and unhappy—like someone channeling Sartre or waiting in line at the post office.

ARE YOU THINKING ABOUT BUYING THAT KERSHISNIK?

I've come close to buying one of Brian's pictures three times: twice from the gallery that represents him and once from a grizzled old coot of a collector who got himself in over his head with his obsessive art purchases and was selling off some things in an effort to save his house. Each time I hesitated. Each time I walked away. Each time I wondered why.

GAVIN?

That was the briefest chat I've had with Gavin in I don't know how long. Mostly we argued about the weather. For all we share, we have radically different ideas about what is and isn't an ideal temperature. Gavin says 81 degrees Fahrenheit; I say 48. This isn't our only difference. Gavin, for example, has high expectations of others and a sense of entitlement—I have neither.

YOU SAID GOODBYE TO RACHEL.

I went down to the laundry room and there she was taking *my* things out of the machine for a change. Of course, I accused her of messing with my underwear. I told her I was leaving, moving out to a place called Winterbrook. She told me she would miss me, then went into a long story about how she was thinking of buying a new car but couldn't decide if this was the time to do it—price and technology-wise. If it was the time to do it, what kind should she buy? She wanted to get a good one, one she looked good in, one that got good gas mileage (because she cared about the environment), but not one with some too-small engine that had no get-up-and-go—though it would probably be better for her if it didn't have any get-up-and-go because her current car has plenty and, as a consequence, she has had several speeding tickets and a threat from her insurance company to drop her if she got another.

IS JESSICA TALKING TO HERSELF?

No, she is just an inveterate chewer of gum.

BED?

There are people who virtually live in bed, who watch television in it, who eat in it, who talk on the phone in it—there are those, I've heard, who write in it. I tried that last night, and it did not work out at all. There are only two things I have ever done in bed. Maybe, if I'm lucky, someday there will be three—maybe, if I'm lucky, I'll die in it. Better than on the bathroom floor.

LAST NIGHT WAS A BIG ONE.

It was. Michael let me sit in on the first rough-cut screening of *Ducks*. He was pleasantly surprised to find what he thought was one of the weakest scenes to be not so bad after all—the flashback scene of a five-year-old Steven in the car with his mother on their way to Seattle.

Other spots didn't fare so well. He didn't care for the scene where Steven sits alone in a coffee shop scanning a newspaper article about the Health and Human Services budget or the meeting-a-clever-beggar-on-the-street scene or the scene in the office where Steven and his beat-up face go to talk with his friend Tim about the psychological pressures that seem to be building in him. I couldn't tell for sure what Michael felt about the thing as a whole, but he seems determined to make what he can out of what he has.

YOU SEEM A LITTLE TENSE?

I always get a little tense on haircut day. I don't like being fiddled with, and I don't like wasting time. Bob, the guy who cuts my hair now, is better than Brenda. He doesn't fuss as much, and he's faster. He doesn't smell as good as Brenda did and he has hairy forearms that tickle the sides of my face when he's cutting on top, but he's better with the small talk. He doesn't make me work as hard, and he doesn't seem inclined to want a "relationship" with me.

WHAT IS BRANDON DOING?

Brandon is decorating his movie about Michael making *his* movie with an assortment of talking-head interviews—mine included. From the questions I've heard him asking, it seems the angle he has chosen is that *Ducks*—while distinctly experimental—is not as experimental as Michael's other movies. Question: Is it possible that Michael has decided to abandon innovation to some degree in search of a larger audience? Zoe Dolnick doesn't think so. She is responsible for makeup, first-aide, and props. She is going to film school and has lots of complex theories about *Ducks*. When she talks, she sounds like she is delivering a term paper: *Ducks* is a departure from convention; it is about challenging the tired tactics of realism; it is an assault on the linear flow of conventional narrative; about cozying up to incoherence, about foregrounding technique, about allowing content to fend for itself, etc., etc., etc.

My feeling, as I tried to explain to Brandon, is that Michael could not, even if he wanted to, give an itemized list of his aesthetic principles—in part because those principles are private and in part because they are unarticulatable. He is not working from theory—though there is certainly some theory thrown in there. Mostly it is just flying by the seat of his artistic pants.

WHO IS THIS ISABELLA HOPPER?

Izzy. She is Carolyn's friend. She was in the neighborhood and thought she would stop by, but no one was answering the door. Jessica (who knows Izzy a little) told her that she had no idea where Carolyn was, but invited her in to wait if she wanted—and she did, for just a few minutes anyway.

Izzy originally met Carolyn when they were in school. Both of them thought they had extrasensory perception and showed up for an experiment that was being conducted in the psychology department. They were asked to transmit selected images telepathically to one another. No luck.

SLEEPLESS NIGHT?

Another lunatic dream not worth repeating—slimy landscape, writhing mutants.

WHERE IS MICHAEL?

Michael has been missing for long stretches these past few days. He has been holed up in a rented editing room working on raw footage trying to make *Ducks Ducks*. It's amazing the number of things that go into making a film a film. It's cutting here and cutting there. It's sound tweaking, adding music, adding voice-overs, adding effects. It is death by micrometers—it is trying to fill a swimming pool using an eyedropper.

WAS THAT A DOG?

Yes. Jessica came home with a dog—a puppy, a blond Labrador. I know this means something, but what? Michael loves dogs, but not the mess. He doesn't like being covered with dog hair and finds it simply incomprehensible that he—so noble in reason, so infinite in faculty, in form and moving so express and admirable—should be expected to follow around behind one picking up its shit.

WHAT ABOUT PANDORA?

(Daniel hunches his shoulders.)

THIS WAS YOUR FAREWELL DINNER.

Just like for my arrival dinner, Jessica made her famous spaghetti. I don't think I turned out to be quite the problem she expected when I moved in. My leaving will be nice, but not as nice as she had originally imagined.

ANOTHER INSTALLMENT OF *ASSISTED LIVING?*

I'm doing a few paragraphs on the summer I spent shoplifting candy bars.

MICHAEL IS HELPING OUT?

Of course. He borrowed Geoff Albee's truck. He is complaining again about my boxes of books. He says I should have fewer and that they should be smaller and not hardbacks.

10

THIS IS A NICE DINING ROOM.

The dining room is the center of Winterbrook culture—just as it was the center of Fairview culture. There are no assigned or designated seats, though over time small cadres of the like-minded have coalesced—the result being some tables that are more open to new members than others. It took a week or so to sort things out—to learn which caucuses to avoid: any including Glen Shields, for instance, and any with the guys who love fishing (and talking about fishing). In general I prefer a table on the periphery, one with a view—which is how I met Anne Hampton, who seems to prefer the same. (The view is across a small garden and into the woods.) Anne has no antipathy for Glen, but she shares my feelings about the fishing buddies. She is the widow of a man who sold mortgage-backed securities for a living.

This is how I met Marilyn Wright as well. She sits where Anne sits. She has a boyfriend at another facility, a place called The Springs. His name is Albert.

She showed me his picture. Long face, fat forehead—he looks like a balding lightbulb.

DOES EVERYONE HAVE AN OPINION ABOUT THE ENTREE?

Everyone here is a learned critic. The beef filet, in addition to being insultingly small, was overcooked and consequently difficult to get through (especially if the teeth you were using were not those given to you by a just and merciful god). The "shaved" potatoes are insufficiently au gratin. The mousse has a chalky aftertaste, etc., etc., etc. The menu writer goes out of his way to make the offerings sound exotically indigenous: there is Oregon veal, Columbia River Salmon, Clatskanie Quail, Willamette Valley Lamb.

WHAT IS THE CURRENT SUBJECT OF CONVERSATION?

The subject of conversation these past few nights has been health-care reform. It is interesting to see who believes who in the debate is lying about what. I am making a list of people (two so far—Allen Hendricks and Barbara Sergeant) who I know for certain I will never be able to have a conversation with about anything.

The real subject, though—the subject everyone is most passionately concerned with—is the burglar. Stuart Weaver, a man usually inclined to talk interminably about his or someone else's golf game, is an expert on the lore. He told us the latest story: how Frank Hodge, who had been down playing checkers with Jerry Parker, was heading back to his room yesterday when he saw someone dressed in black come out of Gilbert Thorne's room and disappear into the stairwell.

THERE WAS A MEETING OF RESIDENTS.

There was. It was called by the manager of the place, Keith Farmer. He said the burglar of Winterbrook was not a rumor, but a confirmed presence. He or she was one of us. He didn't know why this person was doing what they were doing, but they must stop. If he or she continues, he or she will be caught, and once caught, he or she will be expelled—placed back on the looking-for-suitable-accommodations market with a significant black mark against them.

One guy, Donald Kimball—an ex-policeman with hearing and vision issues—has started a sort of patrol.

YOU WERE ASKING ABOUT NATHAN WILSEY?

I haven't seen him in here having a meal. Several people knew who I was talking about, but so far no one I have met has ever actually eaten with him.

WHO IS THAT?

That is Madeline Baker. Every time she sees her grand-children she comments on how big they have gotten. She would like to say something else occasionally, but she can't help herself. Their metamorphosis strikes her as freakish, satanic.

YOU TOOK A WALK WITH ANNE THIS AFTERNOON.

Yes, I did. She showed me the grounds, the special

places where she likes to go to get away from it all. She quizzed me about Emily. I told her what I could—that Emily was, I thought, in France at the moment with our disgruntled son, that we were discussing reconciliation, that it wasn't as farfetched and strange a thing as it might sound, that I was waiting for a reply.

She told me about her dead husband, Bryan.

MORE NOTES FOR *ASSISTED LIVING?*

Yes. Jessica got me thinking about dogs. I'm writing about an old beagle of mine named Toby. He slept by my bed. He had some sort of gastrointestinal disorder and a concomitant inclination to let loose terrible, paint-peeling farts. Trips to the vet were fruitless. Inevitable nightmares—toothed and taloned things tearing me apart. Sleep deprivation. Poor grades.

TED STAVELY FASCINATES YOU.

He does. Every other day or so he shows up at breakfast with a new set of goals in life—ideas about improving himself: drink less, get more exercise, watch his diet, think kinder thoughts about x, y, and z. Things never seem to work out as these various items appear again and again in his repertoire of resolutions.

WHO IS LYDIA POWELL?

She is one of Marilyn's friends. I try to avoid her. She is one of those women who wears too much makeup and is always going on about how good babies smell. She told me a long story about having her purse snatched at the mall. A scruffy looking man just yanked it off her arm and started running. She has to get new credit cards, new library cards, new proof-of-medical-insurance cards, new AAA cards, new grocery-store discount cards, a new driver's license, a new bus pass, a new Social Security card, etc., etc., etc. It is going to take weeks to get her life back in order.

IS THAT A LETTER?

Yes. I'm writing to Lawrence. I told him about our burglar. I suggested he consider setting his next detective novel here. I would be happy to help him with details. I can see his shamus wandering the halls— handsome and mustachioed—the old ladies trailing after him as he hunts down the killer with his side-kick, Luther.

GRAPEFRUIT?

The big discussion here at breakfast is about grape-fruit: is it or is it not dangerous. The worry is about a reputed interaction with certain medications—but which medications, what interaction? No one knows— no one, that is, but John Bloomfield who, since his wife's extended illness, has become something of a pharmacist. According to John, grapefruit juice inter-acts with all sorts of things: antidepressants, antibi-otics, drugs for high blood pressure, drugs to control cholesterol. Reactions depend on the person and their condition—they include muscle pain, fatigue, fever, kidney failure, death.

THE MEMOIR?

Exactly. Back to scribbling—this time about my days working in a bookstore. I thought I knew books pretty well, but I was there six weeks before anyone came in and asked for anything I had even heard of. It was six more weeks before anyone showed up looking for something worthwhile. I don't know what I expected given the nature of the store and its location in the middle of a middling middle-class suburb, but it was something other than that.

WHAT IS GOING ON OUT THERE?

A brouhaha. Roger Booth has attacked Karl Moody with a croquet mallet. The incident is being investigated. A committee is being formed.

11

WHO DID YOU HAVE BREAKFAST WITH?

I had breakfast this morning with Anne and one of her occasional friends, a woman named Sheila.

ISN'T SHE THE ONE WHO EMPLOYS A PSYCHIC?

Yes. One of her regular rituals is to see a psychic on her birthday—which, if I sorted all the clues correctly, was last Wednesday. She is excited because apparently this year's visit has been an especially entertaining one.

HOW SO?

Her psychic—a round-faced woman with long black hair who calls herself Lady Samantha—was in rare form. She told Sheila there would be a worldwide power blackout, two cruise ships would collide in the Caribbean, a cure would be found for the common cold, the Queen of

England would be hospitalized, and a famous Las Vegas hotel-casino would burn to the ground.

ANYTHING ELSE?

Yes. That April would be the best month for her to do any traveling and September the best one for collecting debts.

YOU THINK YOU'RE PSYCHIC?

I do. I knew when Sheila started this story I'd be bored witless before she got to the end of it.

WHAT DID SHEILA SAY ABOUT HER DIVORCE?

She said she thought her interest in psychics played a part in it. I told her one of the things that played a part in mine was my speaking style, which tended to be a little overly succinct. Emily's style was expansive—which was one thing—but it was also repetitive. She liked to go over and over and over a thing. We were often out of sync. Invariably I would be ready to move on in a conversation way before Emily was.

SHEILA MISSED YOUR POINT.

She did indeed.

WHO IS MONICA HEIGHT?

Monica Height is one of those people who has lots of brothers and sisters—seven or eight. This is incomprehensible to me—it must have been like growing up in a commune or a railway station.

WHAT IS THIS HARDEMAN-SIMON STORY ALL ABOUT?

Mrs. Hardeman got into an argument with Mrs. Simon. It got heated to the point that Mrs. Hardeman slapped Mrs. Simon's face. The act caught them both by surprise. Mrs. Simon seems to have gotten over it more or less; Mrs. Hardeman has not. She is still—four days later—mortified. She won't come out of her room.

WHAT WERE YOU ASKING?

I wondered if kids played with marbles anymore? I was asking around. No one seems to know.

YOU ATTENDED THE PREMIERE OF *WILL THERE BE DUCKS* LAST NIGHT?

I did. It was at the Whitsell Auditorium. I ran into Jessica, who was there with Carolyn—both were dressed in black. Jessica was having a little trouble getting into the spirit of things. She was upset about a story in the news—a story about Kashka the giraffe. Apparently a long-time fixture at the Albuquerque zoo, this giraffe died there over the weekend. Some demented zoo worker, rather than doing what protocol dictated in these cases, dismembered the giraffe and tossed him in a nearby dumpster. The remains were discovered and reported by a sanitation worker.

HOW WAS MICHAEL?

Michael is not comfortable in the role of presenter. He does not like talking about the movie much—he prefers it to talk for itself. He feels like a fake, like he is doing some sort of impersonation.

BUT HE TRIED?

He did. He thanked everyone for coming. He said he had his reasons for choosing to handle the film the way he did (the contrapuntal mix of linear and tangled time, for instance), but he had to admit that in part it was sheer cussedness. For one thing, he was hoping "scope" (with a very little "s") might trump a more comfortable cohesion.

WHAT WAS THE RESPONSE TO THE FILM?

It's difficult to characterize the response in general, but it seemed favorable, the applause seemed sincere. The audience seemed to especially like the lantern-smashing-through-the-car-windshield scene and the end, the voice-over "Ducks" speech: "There is some sort of subtle connection being made that suggests this could be the beginning of something. What? Does Steven know? Do you know? What about Amanda and the unrequited love? Will there be ducks where they are going? Will there be a boat?"

SOME OF THE ACTORS WERE THERE.

Most of the people who were in the movie were in the

audience. Only a couple of them had seen it finished. I particularly disliked Miss Stands-Out-In-A-Crowd's date. He was one of those glossy guys.

Joni Travers, who played Amanda, a girl at work who Steven may or may not have been attracted to, complained that Michael had cut out most of her scene. Michael, the diplomat, said it was nothing personal, that he had hated to do it but had been more or less forced to for technical reasons, to tighten certain structural elements.

THAT WASN'T TRUE?

No. In truth he didn't hate to do it at all. He thought her reading was mechanical and her voice almost heliumnated.

MRS. BURKHOLDER IS BOYCOTTING SCRABBLE.

Mrs. Burkholder has stopped playing scrabble with Mrs. Crist because she doesn't like the words Mrs. Crist has been using. They were, according to Mrs. Burkholder, "showoffy." They were words like chimera, mercurial, and ignominious.

WHAT WAS HUGH FENNER TALKING ABOUT?

The more Hugh drinks, the more he talks about living to be one hundred and twenty. We can all live to be one hundred and twenty if we follow his advice—stay in bed, get lots of rest, drink soup, inject HGH (human growth hormone).

PING-PONG?

The room where the ping-pong table sits is perfectly lit—not overdone like Fairview. I devolved from being a reasonably good tennis player into being a very good ping-pong player somewhere in my 50s, and I expected to rank somewhere near the top here at Winterbrook the way I did at Fairview. But then, of course, I hadn't yet met sixty-seven year old Joyce Brown (and her husband, Evan). My second night at the table, I did. She watched me play Don Gilmore. I beat him handily. She asked if I wanted to play her.

AND YOU DID?

I did. There was a warm-up game where she let me stay close. Her squinty-eyed husband, who sat down to watch, signaled her regularly with subtle spasms. She's the talent; he's the strategist.

THERE WAS A WAGER?

Yes. It was Joyce's idea. She said she would play me for my copy of *Cloud Atlas*.

THE DAVID MITCHELL BOOK?

Yes. She saw me reading earlier.

AND?

I asked what would I win. The question caught her completely by surprise—the possibility that this could happen apparently had never really presented itself.

That should have been my first clue. My second clue should have been her walk, which I thought was a bit gym-teacherish.

WHAT DID SHE PUT UP?

She rummaged around in that small suitcase of a purse: I would win an almost-new digital pedometer.

SHE WAS ON?

She was on.

SHE HAD A SLICE.

Joyce's slice to my backhand side was wicked—her clutch shot, the one she fell back on in times of uncertainty (the few that there were). Her height (did you notice she was freakishly tall) made her serve a weapon—the whip-like shenanigans she went through in producing it were very effective. I never knew where the ball was coming from.

SHE WAS ALSO QUICK.

She had a certain flashing quickness that I have to think was medically assisted, but of course I said nothing at the time.

(I mentioned this suspicion to Anne a few days later. She tells me no one who has been here very long will play with her. There is one guy, Mark Draper, who has not been able to reconcile himself to the situation. He keeps trying, but he is the only one.)

JOYCE WON?

She beat me 21-9, 21-8, 21-5 in what I had magnanimously agreed to as a best three-out-of-five series. It was hard to honor her talent as she had a tendency to smile a little too broadly every time she took a point. Also, there was Evan. With each point I could see a little flash—like a tiny firework—go off in his beady eyes.

YOU ARE REASSESSING?

I am. And I'm worried about the effect of this reassessment on my sense of self. You know—unexpected consequences: tiny change here, large change there. A tweak of how I feel about myself as a player of ping pong could lead to a complete reevaluation of my position on capital punishment.

SOMETHING FEELS A LITTLE STRANGE?

Yes. I was wondering about the burglar—if he has been in here. Nothing is missing that I know of, but that does not mean my privacy has not been invaded, my things surreptitiously perused.

POKER NIGHT?

I had the rare privilege of joining in on Wednesday night poker with Peter Lascelles, Charles Voss, and Gary Powell. Gary, rarely raising, took his usual, murderously cautious approach, which got very much on Peter's nerves. He lost to Gary again and again. When he had a high pair, Gary had three Jacks. When he had a straight, Gary had a flush. Peter got wilder and wilder as the night went on—bluffing with abandon, while Gary—smiling that slight, eviscerating smile of his—played a hand only when the stars were aligned.

WHAT WAS JOYCE ASKING YOU ABOUT?

I ran into her in the lobby this morning. She was reading her prize. She wanted to talk to me about the book, about the profusion of stories, what did I think . . . She pretended it was an innocent question and that she was not just trying to rub it in—the ownership of *Cloud Atlas*.

WHAT DID YOU SAY?

I said Mr. Mitchell was a writer of preternatural facility and abundance, that he was an enigma to me, that the book was a linguistic extravaganza, but that I had found I didn't really have a lot to say about it after "wow." I told her I could not figure out why a book this good didn't really matter to me the way it (being a book this good) should, but in the end, alas—if I was going to be honest with her—I would have to say it didn't.

THAT WAS SEVERE.

My reservations say more about me than about Mr. Mitchell. I don't think there is any question that he is a true great.

YOU ARE BACK ON *ASSISTED LIVING?*

I am. I was working on some notes about a brief flirtation with therapy a few years back. It wasn't long after Emily left. I was, understandably I think, a bit down. For a while I kept going down. I found myself talking to fewer and fewer people for shorter and shorter amounts of time—I had a sense I might be disappearing into the reclusive weirdness that has always summoned me, so I asked around. I got the name of a doctor from a guy in my department at Greenhurst, a Henry James scholar who was known to have flamed-out and recovered three separate times. This doctor, Andrew Culver, had done wonders with him—maybe he could help me.

IT DIDN'T WORK OUT?

No. I went three or four times. I talked about my life and about what I thought was bothering me, but there was one thing I found I could not go into—namely, that one of the things bothering me was him.

DR. CULVER?

Yes. There were several things I did not care for about him. One of them was the writing. He scribbled incessantly as I talked. I had to slow down for him all the time. I got the feeling he was not really listening to what I was saying, not transcribing answers, but working on some sort of crossword puzzle.

From the conversations we had when he was not scribbling, I could see he was determined to convince me that I did not know what my feelings really were about this and that. My world was confused enough. I didn't really need to start doubting what I felt.

I don't t know what I think; therefore, I am not. That was my Cartesian interpretation.

YOU SAW MARILYN?

Yes. She was sitting out in the garden alone this afternoon staring off into space. She looked lost and woebegone.

12

AND WHO DID YOU HAVE BREAKFAST WITH THIS MORNING?

I had breakfast this morning with Anne and Hillary.

HILLARY?

Hillary Gidden, another one of Anne's collected acquaintances. She was upset about her new glasses. She thought they looked good in the shop and the woman who waited on her said they did, but she could see now that they were too emphatic and the wrong shape—they made her face look too round. She was going to have to take them back, but she didn't want to because the woman who waited on her hadn't actually been very nice. Hillary couldn't figure out exactly why—there was just something about her that apparently rubbed this woman the wrong way. She wouldn't have gone to this shop in the first place, but it was close and had good prices and Sheila, who has a very nice pair of glasses, recommended it.

WHAT IS GOING ON OVER THERE?

There is a small gathering every afternoon of men and women with insurance forms. They get together in the hope of helping one another. Occasionally there is an accountant or some sort of ersatz linguist, but they are never a match for the task. The questions and answers usually start off simple and straightforward enough, but before long things get out of hand and the meeting devolves into a moil of frustration—part stipulative scrum, part séance—a cacophony of tangled interpretations, imprecations, and calculations.

THE BURGLAR HAS STRUCK AGAIN.

Yes. The Winterbrook Burglar—he (or she) has struck again. They have taken a pewter flask from John Bryson.

ISN'T HE THE ONE WHO JUMPS ROPE?

Yes. He's an interesting guy. He jumps rope to ward off depression. He has cleared a large space in the middle of his living room for this. He tripped himself up the other day and had a nasty fall. He was kept in the hospital overnight for observation, When he came home he found the flask was missing. It was part of his flask collection. It once belonged to Winston Churchill and is supposed to be valuable.

THERE ARE THEORIES.

One of the theories floating around is about the woman from housekeeping, the one that does this floor. She has a limp and, judging from her complexion, a vitamin deficiency. The limp is a leftover from a domestic dispute—she was shot in the leg by her boyfriend. She makes a lot of people here uncomfortable with her greenish skin and her involvement in violence. Several of the women here—Sheila being one of them—say she flirts with John and with Malcolm Fulford—both widowers with money who probably don't have that much longer to live. They wouldn't put burglary past her.

ASSISTED LIVING?

At some point I am going to have to take a stab at a summary statement. I can't imagine right now what it will be. I suspect it will be some sort of ode to ignorance—a tribute suggesting the increased awareness of one's own idiocy that accrues with age is in the end the true fount of wisdom.

IS JANET WHATELY NEW TO WINTERBROOK?

Yes, she is. She still doesn't know quite what to make of the place. She has lived most of her life in a small room with bad wallpaper.

DESCRIBE HER.

She is the sort of woman who likes egg salad sandwiches.

YOU TOOK A LITTLE WALK AROUND THE POND.

I did. I had a headache. I thought a walk around the pond might help. It has in the past.

AND DID IT HELP THIS TIME?

Some. The path, however, is covered in several critical places with goose poop. There is no option but to walk in it. Sort of like life, I think.

I am sure I will hear from Emily next week or the week after about the proposed reconciliation. We will get it worked out. The negotiations continue.

IS THAT THE FIRST REVIEW OF MICHAEL'S MOVIE?

It is.

AND?

And it is basically what he expected: a complaint that *Ducks* is not the film the reviewer would have preferred it to be, a complaint that Michael has sacrificed what is automatically assumed to be the holy grail of these exercises—emotional engagement—for the sake of a few intellectually diverting tricks.

AND?

The traditional grumbles about Michael's interest in the devices of filmmaking as being *di rigueur*—the fragmented presentation, for instance; the playing around with the illusion of reality in service to the illusion of reality; the brief intrusions of a character called "the filmmaker" played with conspiratorial aplomb by the cleft-chinned ham, James Foster.

Michael took it in stride. He wondered why this man had even bothered seeing the thing. It was probably an assignment.

MRS. MCCARTHY IS SOAKING WET.

She is known for taking walks in the rain. She doesn't care if she ruins her hairdo. In my experience here, that makes her unique.

WHAT IS THE MATTER? YOU DON'T LOOK HAPPY?

Hard time working on my notes tonight. Inexplicably disheartened. I do not seem to be the dedicated person I once was. I can only hope it is a phase.

WHAT WAS THAT ALL ABOUT?

There was considerable excitement at breakfast. Apparently Mrs. Carter found a spider in her bed. Mr. Carter (who bludgeoned the thing to death with a flashlight) has looked her over from top to bottom, and it does not appear she has been bitten. They will continue to monitor the situation. You can never be too careful when it comes to spiders.

WHO WAS THAT AT THE DOOR?

Alan Estes and Paul Vlassic. They want to know if I am interested in joining them in the community room. There is a recital this evening by the Chapman Quartet;

they are doing excerpts from Brahms, Rachmaninoff, and Tchaikovsky.

WHAT DID YOU SAY?

I told them I might be down later, but I had to make a call (to Lawrence).

AND THE TWO OF THEM JUST STOOD THERE?

Yes, they did. I asked if there was something else? Paul wanted to know what I thought about the latest Winterbrook burglary. I told him I would talk to him about it later. "Well, shall we go," Paul says—to which Alan replies, "Yes, let's." And away they went.

Lawrence was not home. I hadn't actually expected him to be.

DID YOU ENJOY THE RECITAL?

It was okay. It, of course, made me think of Gavin— the quintessential interpreter of the baroque violin. We have been friends all this time because we share so many traits—reclusiveness, a generalized anxiety, stubbornness, insomnia, a proneness to bouts of exhausting intensity. There was a period when I was obsessed with him, I think; his bizarre life with its uncompromising devotion to the art that maintained him seemed to be a model one to me. There is a part of me that still looks at him as the embodiment of some sort of ideal, but now there is another part that is suspicious of that part. If Emily were aware of the true depth of my admiration for Gavin she would not like it (Gavin represents pathology to her), but if she knew about the new way I feel, I have to think it would make a difference.

There is a man named Haskell who wrote a terrific short story about Glenn Gould, the neurotic Canadian virtuoso who reminds me very much of Gavin. He talked about Gould's fear of death. He mentioned a line from Shakespeare's *The Tempest*—a line Gould would have known. Prospero is talking about death. He says, "Every third thought shall be my grave." Haskell says that that was the way it was with Gould—Book. Beer. Death. Lamp. Coat. Death, etc., etc., etc. For a while after the "apparent" heart attack, "death and dying" was my every third thought, too. But I'm improving. It became my every fourth thought, then my every fifth, then my every sixth. Now it is something like my every twenty-fifth. (I guess you would say it went something like this: light, water, radio, lather, razor, teeth, vitamins, socks, shoes, curtains, newspaper, mug, coffee, bowl, cereal, milk, spoon, dishwasher, keys, wallet, glasses, cash, door, car, death.) I will be back on dry land, so to speak, when it gets to being my every one-hundredth. I want to stay aware enough to fully appreciate what I have, but not so aware as to spoil it. Proportion is a tricky thing.

WHO IS THAT?

Dan Noakes. He has a weakness for taffy-colored shoes.

Appendices

Appendix 1

Richard Introduces Himself
by
Peter Brooks

Thank you. I was going to say it was nice to be here, but of course you know it isn't. Not really. I mean it is better to be here than nowhere, but…well, you know what I'm getting at. I can tell by all that headshaking.

I guess I should start with my name—it's Richard. I was born in Baltimore, Maryland, but I don't really make a big deal out of it. As I understand it, there are people who do. I can't imagine why. Maybe we could discuss that later.

So what first…my unremarkable childhood I suppose. It was pretty much normal as far as I can tell. I grew up wearing ugly T-shirts and loving all the stuff I was supposed to—ice cream, playing outside, television. I got my first spanking at the age of five (for punching my sister in the stomach) and my first dog at the age of eight. His name was Barney. He was run over by a neighbor with a low IQ.

At ten I wanted to be a scientist. I was particularly interested in rockets. I built them from kits. My father would take me out Saturday mornings to a nearby park and let me shoot them off. These rockets were powered by small gunpowder-filled engines that looked like rolls of quarters. At the top of each engine was a small reverse-blast section. Once the fuel was burned up in the ascent, this back-blast would blow the nosecone off the rocket allowing a small, colorful parachute to deploy.

One afternoon when I was home alone, I decided to launch one of these rockets from my backyard. It went astray. It lost a tailfin at blastoff and corkscrewed across the street. It flew into the Kelby's house and stuck in the livingroom ceiling. When the back-blast went off it started a fire in the attic.

In high school I took an interest in acting. Because I had a good memory and a natural scowl, I was given the part of Iago in a thoroughly lackluster production of *Othello*. At our final dress rehearsal I had an accident. I was struggling with a speech in Act 2 when I stepped off the stage and fell into the orchestra pit. I landed on my head, getting a concussion, a gash above my eye, and the first of three rides I have had in ambulances. There was talk of the school having been negligent. A settlement was made.

I had my first coital experience at the age of sixteen—though I frequently lie about this and claim to have had it at the age of twelve. The object of my affection was a shiny blond girl named Shelly. We were together for almost two years.

In college I fell under the influence of a professor by the name of Maywood and became a Platonist. I rented a small studio apartment, ate nothing but raisins and yogurt, and sought to live a life devoted to the contemplation of eternal truths. I was well on the way to achieving self-mastery when I met Pamela Hershey. She popped up out of the English Department in a tight yellow sweater and introduced into my life some eloquent arguments for the primacy of passion. We moved into a little cottage that was paneled with knotty pine. Six months later she found someone with a more arbitrary sense of fun.

When I graduated I took a job as a statistical analyst for a company that sold burglar alarms. I tracked national crime rates and reported what I found to our sales and marketing departments. I did this for almost three years. I quit when I realized my daily immersion in this pond of toxic numbers had transformed me from a relatively calm and confident individual into a highly agitated and fearful one. I developed a drinking problem and went to Arizona for eight weeks to recover.

When I returned I was a new man. I was dried out and in touch with my transcendent side. I took a job with a company that published investment newsletters. I was with them for almost a year, but left when a disagreement about just what did and did not constitute ethical business practices got out of hand and I was put in the position of having to say some things that nobody really wanted to hear.

I have been in my new position at Fidelity Insurance for almost a month now and am enjoying it very much. Each morning at 9:45 a.m. I wander down to the second floor lunchroom where I get myself a piece of gooey apple strudel. By an expensive and time-consuming process of elimination, I have determined this strudel to be the most consistently palatable thing to be found in the Fidelity vending machines. Sealed in cellophane, it's folded over like a wallet and decorated with gravelly grains of sugar. I recommend it to anyone who might be interested.

Appendix 2

Coffee Girl
by
Phillip Thaw

How many times have we sat here almost next to each other and not said a word. I don't know. Too many. Please don't mistake my silence for anything other than what it is— which is just me being the way I am at this hour of the day.

* *

Yes, I saw you reading the newspaper this morning. How could I not. To be honest with you, I'd have to say that look of concentration struck me as a bit contrived. I could be wrong. Maybe you're as interested in the plight of the Palestinians as you're supposed to be. I was tempted to ask for the sports section, but I didn't because I knew you'd recognize the gesture for what it was and think me pathetic.

* *

You sip your cappuccino casually but I can tell from the barely detectable twitching of the muscles in your face that you continue to worry about the nature of our relationship and that you are, in fact, worried about this worrying because you think of yourself as someone who is worldly and sophisticated. I don't really think this obsessing is something you object to deep down nearly as much as you claim. I think you object to it, at least in part, because you think I object to it.

* *

Today I am wearing my black shirt and my black pants, and I can see you are dazzled by my uptown snazziness but at the same time made uneasy because you were under the impression that we had somehow tacitly agreed to arrive here looking a certain way and I've suddenly arrived looking like this, like someone else completely, and you have not. I can feel you fighting the urge to say something hurtful and sarcastic to me.

* *

I noticed you notice me noticing the girl in the magazine ad. You think I am attracted, but I'm not. I mean, yes, she is beautiful and I'm sure some strangely named part of my brain has been stimulated by the sight of her, but I'm more antagonized than aroused. I mean, yes, her hair shines and tumbles fetchingly over her shoulders, and, yes, her eyes are set farther apart than yours, and, yes, she can press her lips together in such a way as to look simultaneously amused and complex—but that attitude of pampered distain she seeks to convey…it completely ruins her for me.

⁂

I can't explain it but for some reason I have the distinct impression you like the smell of me.

⁂

I saw you trying to listen in on that conversation—the one between the girl who always slouches down in her chair and the one with the scary blue fingernails. What did you expect to hear—something about the affair the one who always slouches down in her chair was having with her minty-breathed dentist or something about the one the girl with the scary blue fingernails was having with the pigeon-toed banker who likes to sing Bob Dylan songs in the shower?

⁂

No, I am not offended by the suggestion that I grow a beard. I've thought about it before but not very seriously because (1) I don't think it would be a very good beard and (2) there would probably be too much red in it. I know you have taken a vote and that several of your friends have agreed with you, but I'm afraid that doesn't really incline me to do it.

❦

I can tell by the way you are staring out the window that you're not thinking about me. You're just looking at whatever it is that's going on out there and ignoring it. Funny, it seems such a private moment to have in such a public place.

❦

The guy at the cash register is trying his best to be irresistible. He says something to you about it being a small world and it reminds you of what…Disneyland, I think. Any other day you would have followed this recollection— you would have remembered the time when you were visiting and your brother (who always ruined everything for you) got sick and had to be rushed to the hospital with a burst appendix. (You sat in the waiting room picking cotton candy out of your hair while he was being x-rayed. To make the time go by you wrote a postcard home to your dog Boots who was locked up without his ball in your grandparents' bleak basement.) But not today…you don't follow this recollection today. Today you let it go where it will. You wash your hands of it. You think instead about your checkbook and its refusal to balance…about your reading glasses, which you must replace because whatshisname, that behemoth from accounting, has dropped his massive briefcase on them.

I think you are waiting for someone. You have that look. Who is it? Is it that friend of yours who was arrested for shoplifting shoes—the one who wants to lose weight, clean up her apartment, get a better job, and improve her personality. The one who wears her clothes too tight—whose head squeezes up out of the top of her turtleneck like a dab of toothpaste out of a tube.

Do you remember the night I was going to tell you about when it was raining and unpleasant out and I was feeling sort of sick to my stomach so I stayed home listening to the strange noises my refrigerator makes. I listened to them for hours until I sort of put myself into a trance. When I came out of it I felt different, confused—the way you feel when you come home from the ocean.

You think I've withdrawn even further into myself than usual today, that I am focusing on some personal peculiarity that I have embraced as being the essence of that which makes me special and knowing. You think it's your job to play along, that I will be charmed by your willingness to champion the unconventional, that we will be knowing and special together. You think it will be amusing to whisper forbidden things.

＊＊

This morning we play some sort of game that involves the making and breaking of eye contact. At the end we have that moment—that frozen, ten-second-thick sliver of forever that is almost Swedish in its enigmatic ambiguity. It hangs there in the air like some fancy special-effects revenant—something that suggests something about whatever it is that is going on between us—a phantasmagorical piñata stuffed with insinuation that we invite our eager chroniclers to attack with flattering interpretations.

＊＊

I don't think you are as unconcerned today as you pretend. The future is not so distant as to feel like never.

Appendix 3

Will There Be Ducks?
by
Kevin Richardson

What do you think when you first see him? Not much. You think we must be moving on to someone else, someone you could recognize ten minutes from now if you had to, someone with a little more character in his face, someone with some lines here and there, someone with an unusual nose or one of those cleft chins. But no, this is him. Steven. Steven Skidmore. Mr. Easy-Not-To-Notice, Mr. Likes-His-Carbohydrates, Mr. Nothing Special. Look at that sad tie. Is this Everyman? Is that what I'm up to here? What if I say he was born in Nebraska. Do I need to say anything else? Do I need to say he's white? Do I need to say he is 35 years old? Do I need to say he believes in beef, baseball, and straight talking—that he is, on some level, embarrassed to be feeling rarified, unmanly things?

What does the bar look like? It looks like the Kingston

before they remodeled. Lots of dark wood and scuffed vinyl. A warm, yeasty-smelling place—a place where lots of things are sticky that shouldn't be.

He's thinking about what—all the money he owes, how he hates his job, how he wishes Randall, the guy in the cubicle next to him, would say something interesting for just once in his life?

※ ※

When he leaves the bar is he drunk? A little, maybe. Certain things come closer than usual to making sense, and he's more likely than he might otherwise have been to be precise in the sentences he imagines. So how does he get hit in the face? Does he run into someone in the parking lot—a feral, predatory youth, the sort we like to hold up as an example to others of just what can happen when mothers are drug-addicted or teachers insufficiently nurturing— someone pierced and tattooed, a player of hacky sack, a haver of bad attitudes? No. He clips a light pole as he is driving out of the parking lot.

A light pole?

He's distracted. Someone he has seen in the bar has reminded him vaguely of Pamela Engebretson, a girl he knew in high school. He is mesmerized for a moment by the vividness of what he can remember—the shade of her tan, the texture of her favorite sweater, the beadiness of her optometrist father's eyes. He is trying to say her name out loud when he turns a little too sharply and catches the pole with twenty-five pounds of classic American-made front bumper, snapping it at the base. The lantern part of the light—a thing roughly the size and shape of a rural mailbox—comes smashing through the windshield of his sad little rattletrap. It happens quickly and is a complete surprise to everyone.

* *

Steven drives off.

Can we hear what is playing on his radio as we watch the glow of his taillights recede into the distance? Maybe. It's that song by whatshisname, isn't it? The one Nick has identified as "spine tingling," capable of making a person question his unquestioning faith in the literal.

Is this sudden confrontation with fortuity an intimation of things to come? Is it the spark that starts some sort of psychic and/or thematic fire? Is it the sort of thing a reader's guide might refer to: "In the opening of the story, Steven Skidmore, the main character, is hit in the face by a falling lamp. What is the significance of this 'accident'?"

* *

Does Steven have anyone waiting for him at home—anyone who could or would help him pick the glass out of his face? No. Not since "she" (whose name we do not mention) moved out.

So?

So he drives his lonesome, battered, bloodied self to the nearest hospital emergency room where he is treated expeditiously and released.

* *

How do Kathy and Christine act when Steven walks into the office the next morning? Just as you would imagine.

Steven tries to pass off his swollen, stitched-up hideousness as nothing really worth talking about, but Kathy, who has an appetite for life and can't help herself, wants a full plate of details so he invents an 80-year-old woman, an intersection, and a 1996 pearl-white Cadillac Seville with automatic transmission and leather seats.

Do Kathy and Christine have auto accident stories of their own to tell? Of course.

Kathy's involves a rear-end collision in which her little dog, a shiatsu named Suzie, is thrown into the dashboard and knocked out. (When it awakens it has a completely different personality.)

And Christine's? Christine's involves the death of a child—a cousin's son. He was seven. What is Steven thinking as he listens to her? Does he recall some tragic incident in his own life—a younger brother drowned in the backyard pool, a pretty neighbor girl inadvertently poisoned? Is that what this is about—a buried and deforming pain? Is he wearing the right facial expression for someone listening to such a story? What should he say? How can people tell you something like this? What do they want? Can it be provided? How will he fail them?

* *

What about the backstory? Who is Everyman? Where did he go to school? What sort of jobs did he have before he ended up with this one? He used to be one way, now he's another. Does he know why?

Next morning. The alarm clock goes off. Is he a heavy sleeper or an insomniac?

Trying to shave around all of his cuts and stitches is a challenge. With all that swelling and his nose still pointing off in the wrong direction, he can barely recognize himself—he looks like some sort of laboratory experiment gone wrong. As he stares at the mess in front of him he remembers his first fistfight. It was with a boy named Alan Peacock. What was it about? He has no idea. He does, however, remember wishing it had been with someone else, someone more popular, someone more coordinated, someone whose defeat would have bequeathed him greater honor.

What is sitting there on the counter for us to see? A ceramic cup, a soap dispenser, a radio. He turns on NPR and listens to a story about what? About a cinnamon bun that looks like Mother Teresa. It has been stolen from a coffeehouse in Nashville. Steven remembers Nashville. He drove through it once when he was five. He was in a station wagon with his mother. She was smoking and talking non-stop about the miraculous new life they were going to have in Seattle.

What was he thinking about as he watched the highway flying by? He was thinking about the life he was leaving behind, a life where he and his friends used to chase each other for no reason, where they used to throw oranges at the ghosts in his grandmother's garage. And? And he was wondering about the new life—the one he was heading toward. Was there going to be anything to do in it, anyone to do it with? Would it be a life of cereal that was good for him, a life spent in the kitchen listening to his mother cry in front of the stove? Would there be ducks where they are going? Would there be a boat?

**

Steven is sitting at his desk. He looks overwhelmed by the insignificant day-in day-out sameness of his job. He stares silently into space as he taps a mock SOS on the keyboard of his computer. Is this a story about the mysterious workings of the human heart, about the disastrous consequences of a failure to ignore the logical conclusions that have been made inevitable by the spirit of the age?

**

At home we watch him make what sort of dinner for himself? Is it some sad little frozen thing like a potpie or an elaborate, gourmetish production that involves lots of fancy preparation and expertise? What about coriander and cumin? It would be nice, wouldn't it, to have their scents seep into a paragraph.

Later he sits down in front of the television. He has a beer. What is he watching? Should it be something that has some sort of oblique connection to the theme of the story or something that suggests the previously unsuggested?

More deep, quiet regret. Is he a man pursued by a knowledge of his limitations? Look at the way he sits: it's the classic posture of defeat. What is he thinking? Is it about Laura who he lived with for six months? Laura who started working on a committee to save Mill Pond, who started coming home late. Laura who for some reason didn't seem excited about him any more, who stopped answering his questions, who started getting telephone calls that were difficult to explain. Laura who moves out and takes his most flattering estimation of himself with her.

Is this story about loneliness? What about fate? Identity? Being enlightened? What about pitiless truth-telling, a decent man's passage, the mystery of things as they should be? What about the case for counting cats in Zanzibar?

⁂

The lantern—a thing roughly the size and shape of a rural mailbox—has smashed through his windshield. He has driven off. What if he just stays on the road? What if he drives and drives until there is only blackness, until he runs out of gas? What if he sits in his car at the side of the road until someone passing stops to ask if he is ok? If he doesn't answer what would happen? Who would be called? Would he be lifted out of the front seat by large men? Would he be placed on a stretcher? Where would he be taken?

⁂

Morning. Steven is in a coffee shop about a block from his office. He is sitting alone with a cup of espresso, not noticing anything around him, reading a piece of newspaper he has taken from the empty table next to him. What is the story? Is it about the Department of Human Services budget, the new Opera Center, the kidnapped coed?

**

He runs into Gary Doyle at the elevator. Does he know
him very well? No. Gary works in credit.

What floor?

Six, please.

Apropos of nothing, Gary brings up the subject of what?
His son. Apparently he has just won a prize at his school's
science fair. His project involved measuring the amount of
bacteria to be found in various samples of ice.

**

And what about Amanda in order production? Does he
have a little thing for her? She is a doctor's daughter. She
went to an expensive school and is now living with an over-
weight man who refinishes wood floors for a living. How
does she feel about Steven? She seems to like him, but she
seems to like everybody. Is this what the story is about—
Steven's unrequited feelings for Amanda? A little late to
introduce her isn't it? How big are her eyes? What color
is her hair? What does he want to say to her? He wants to
say something that cuts through the trivial, something that
takes a chip out of the foundation of a significant proposition—but in a funny way. He wants to say something that
will make her think and laugh. Something that will make
her respect him. He wants to say something that could
make a difference were the situation somehow other than
what it was.

**

Maybe he should go for a walk at lunch. It would be good to get him outside where the wonders of nature could be anthropomorphized and the reader alerted to the author's ungrudging reverence for a certain type of award-winning prosody. The leaves on the trees could be curling at the corners like coy but villainous smiles. The clouds could glide across the distant horizon like so many gossamer galleons. Maybe this would be the place to put the panhandler—the one with the fishing pole. Steven stops and gives him something. How much? Not much. He saves his silver for later. (Each afternoon at 2:15 p.m. he wanders down to the lunchroom where he gets himself a carton of milk and a bag of chocolate chip cookies.)

※ ※

Steven walks into Tim Cumming's office to complain about yet another pointless report he has been asked to put together by someone I will probably call Davidson. Why is he really here? He is really here because certain pressures seem to be building. His face hurts. His landlady hates him. He is being devoured at night by his very own Steven-ness. Things seem to be going places even though he doesn't want them to, and he thinks Tim, being the sort of person he is—an obviously-troubled-but-still-together sort—might be able to help. And is he? Not really.

Steven tries to steer the conversation toward what are to him the pertinent issues but is unsuccessful as Tim is preoccupied with a jammed stapler and a detailed account of his latest recurring nightmare.

⁂

Saturday. He has gone to an early movie and is now following a girl he noticed there as she walks off down the street. It is some sort of game he has decided to play with himself—a test. A test of what? Does he know? Does the reader know?

What do you think when you first see her? You think she must be the one. Why even look anywhere else? This is her: Miss Stands-Out-In-A-Crowd, Miss Watches-Her-Weight, Miss Cleaner-Than-Clean. What if I said she was born in California? Do I need to say anything else? Do I need to say she is blonde? Do I need to say she is 22? Do I need to say the air around her is different than the air around everyone else?

Steven follows her into a card shop. She is buying what—a birthday card for her mother. Pretending to be looking at cards himself, he gets close enough to read the one she is holding: "No matter where life may lead me, I'll always be thankful for who you are." Really? No. This girl's mother has told her terrible things about her father, things a truly special mother would never tell a daughter. She has destroyed part of the girl's memory of him because he never made her as happy as she felt she deserved to be.

What about Steven's mother? Was he thankful for who she was? No. An alcoholic suicide, he had to stop feeling much about her one way or the other a long time ago.

In getting close enough to read the card Steven has made the girl nervous and uneasy. His battered face suggests what to her? Cravenness? Criminality? She knows he has followed her. Does she say anything to him? Maybe she tries to inch away. Maybe she goes to the woman behind the cash register and asks for help. Is a security person called? Is that what this story is about—Steven devolving before our eyes into something creepy?

Does he do something theatrical here—something denouement-like? Does he try to kiss the girl and get wrestled to the ground and handcuffed? Does this become a story about doing hard time, about drooling cellmates with hairy backs and rustic diction? Or does he do something smaller, something into which just about anything can be read? Maybe he just walks off into the sunset? Can we hear what he is whistling? It's that song by whatshisname, isn't it? The one Nick has identifiedas "spine tingling," capable of making a person question his unquestioning faith in the literal. What about something midway between big and little? Maybe he introduces himself to the girl and apologizes just before the guard arrives. He tells her that she reminds him of someone. He tells her about the parking lot, about getting hit in the face, about the lantern—a thing roughly the size and shape of a rural mailbox. They go for a cup of coffee. There is some sort of subtle connection being made that suggests this could be the beginning of something. What? Does he know? Does the reader know? What about Amanda? Will there be ducks where they are going? Will there be a boat?

www.ingramcontent.com/pod-product-compliance
Lightning Source LLC
Chambersburg PA
CBHW021203110726
47900CB00002B/713